OLIVIA SAMMS

SKETCHY

THE BEA CATCHER CHRONICLES: BOOK 1

AMAZON CHILDREN'S PUBLISHING

For my mom.
"Sing for us, Janet!"

Amazon Publishing
Attn: Amazon Children's Publishing
P.O. Box 400818
Las Vegas, NV 89140
www.amazon.com/amazonchildrenspublishing

ISBN-13: 9781477816509 (hardcover)
ISBN-10: 147781650X (hardcover)
ISBN-13: 9781477866504 (eBook)
ISBN-10: 1477866507 (eBook)

Book design by Sammy Yuen
Editor: Marilyn Brigham

Printed in The United States of America (R)
First edition
10 9 8 7 6 5 4 3 2

It was the pom-pom the boys spotted first. The metallic strands were tangled around a batch of tall cattails. The rain-soaked cheerleading skirt, hung to dry, was draped over a wild lilac bush. A size 7-1/2 white tennis shoe lay wedged in mud at their feet, at the edge of the creek.

The boys, sophomores at Packard High School in Ann Arbor, Michigan, were cutting class. Mason got a hold of what he thought was some weed. Joey was pissed at his mom and dad for grounding him that weekend over a bad grade on a chemistry test. So they cut PE, lunch, and study hall—not really classes, they justified—hiked down to the creek a mile west of the school, and lit up some oregano-laced pencil shavings.

Believing he indeed felt a buzz, Mason untangled the lone, soaked pom-pom from the cattails. "Stand up, sit down, fight, fight, fight, fight!"

Joey snorted with laughter and held the cheerleading skirt up to his body, kicking his legs high into the air until he tripped on the muddy tennis shoe. He fell, his knees hitting the wet ground first. His upper body followed—his head slapping against the cold, pale flesh of her right thigh.

She was on her back at the edge of the creek, lying beneath an old, wooden, waterlogged canoe. Only her bruised legs were exposed—splayed, one bent over the other, posed in a twisted triangle.

Joey jumped up and vomited. "Oh my god, what the fuck is that? Who is that?"

Mason inched his way over to the body. He snapped off a branch from the thicket, poked at the rotted canoe, and pushed it toward the water. The wood broke apart, splintering, floating away downstream like a group of innocent bystanders.

Her torso was wrapped in a moldy blanket. Her head was tilted to the side, her neck swollen with red welts and bruises. Her normally sleek blond hair was now brown, caked with mud and strewn across her face like a dirty mop. Her eyes were blindfolded with a black scarf.

"Is that who I think it is? Is she . . . is she fucking dead?" Joey asked.

Mason bent down, pulled her hair off her face, and lifted the scarf from her eyes. He placed his fingers on her neck, below her ear, feeling for a pulse.

Willa blinked a swollen, bloodshot eye at him and grabbed his ankle.

I am fifteen minutes late, and I feel like everyone is staring at me. *Please, please don't look at me—I don't want to be here. I don't belong here,* I silently scream to them. I'm seventeen and should be out with friends, having a good time, doing stupid shit that only seventeen-year-olds do.

Oh yeah, that's what got me in trouble in the first place—the stupid shit.

I find an empty metal folding chair in the back row and sit, hoping the meeting will continue on, but the chair squeaks on the linoleum floor as I scoot it forward. One of the fine-tipped pens holding up my piled, black kinky nest of hair falls to the ground. I pick it up, and the dozen silver bangles on my wrist jangle. My sketchbook falls out of my vintage-sixties fringed handbag with a thud. *So much for sneaking in the back.*

They continue to stare, and the mediator—the man in the front of the room, wearing a ridiculous Hawaiian shirt—says, "Welcome! Aloha!" He smiles and nods at me like an idiot bobblehead, and he waits. They all wait for the words I don't want to say.

Fuck it—whatever. "My name is Bea, and I'm an addict and alcoholic."

I hate those words and only say them because I'm ordered to—an order enforced by this ridiculous "club" that I've found myself thrown into because of my parents.

"Hello, Bea. I understand you get your three-month chip today." Hawaiian-shirt man smiles. Everyone in the room claps as he walks over and hands me a cheap-looking plastic chip. I roll my eyes and drop it into my purse.

They're all phonies—plastic, like the chip—a bunch of losers. A housewife in khakis two sizes too small; a grandma in a muumuu that no doubt smells of mothballs; a trucker guy wearing a wifebeater—all sitting under the flickering, fluorescent lights of St. Anne's recreational hall. Strong coffee percolates in the back kitchen; it stinks of despair.

They continue on with their own dramas and leave me alone, so I settle in as best I can, crack open my Moleskine sketchbook, a new one from my dad, look at the time on my phone, and write:

3 months

19 hours

21 minutes . . . sober

Hello new sketchbook :)
Welcome to my life . . . Beatrice Washington's
horrible, crappy, sucky life!
Thankfully I am out of rehab—finally—
but my first night of freedom? A stupid AA meeting!
aka . . . ASSHOLES ANONYMOUS

I spot a couple of smokers at an open side door, polluting the crisp, clean, autumn Michigan air, unable to tear themselves away from their nicotine fix for even an hour. One of the guys is cute—in his twenties or late teens, like me. Regardless, he's more my type than the lowlifes who fill the hall. And I haven't seen a member of the opposite sex my age, especially a cute one, for more than three months.

I try to get his attention. I concentrate on his shaggy brown hair, his wide-set eyes that squint when he inhales his cigarette. I *will* him to look at me. *LOOK AT ME, GOD DAMMIT*. I blow it out to him like a paranormal cloud of smoke. *Look at me now! Look! At! Me!*

But he doesn't.

I think about joining him for a smoke (having picked up the habit at rehab). But I'd probably trip or something, attracting more attention, more stares, and more judgment. And that is *so* not what I want. What I want is to wake up from this nightmare and have the last three months of my life back.

But since I don't possess the supernatural power of time travel, I will try and make the best of the hour, make myself more comfortable by placing my leather bomber jacket that I bought at the flea market for thirty-five bucks under my butt for extra padding.

> I'm sitting between a granny knitting baby booties and a trucker with major BO. He's sound asleep . . . drooling and snoring, gross!

A redheaded woman walks up to the front. She's one of the younger ones in this morgue—in her late twenties—and she thinks she's hot, you can tell. You know, big boobs, big hair, and tons of tats. But her look obviously works for the trucker next to me, as he suddenly wakes with a start and sits on the edge of his folding chair, lapping up every word coming out of her crooked, pencil-lined lips.

Her name is Karin, she says, "with an *i* instead of an *e*." She giggles, like she's just made a joke. "And I've been clean for four years now."

Applause from the losers. The trucker goes nuts and slaps his dirty paws together, almost hitting me.

Fearing for my safety, I move my chair away from him and a bit closer to granny (I was right about the mothballs), and I begin to doodle in my sketchbook. Karin "with an *i* instead of an *e*" continues on with her story. She chokes up a little. I look at her and think, *Is that really necessary?*

In an instant, the image of a sleeping kid barrels through

my head. It starts at the back of my eyeballs and fills my brain, shoots down my right arm, and possesses my hand, and I draw the sleeping child as Karin continues, sharing with us the reason she is here at St. Anne's church on this shitty October night in Ann Arbor, Michigan.

"My rock bottom? When one of my tricks beat my face in—yeah, smashed my nose, broke a cheekbone. It was horrible getting beat up. But the worst part was when I got home. I forgot to call the babysitter and found my three-year-old asleep in my bed—alone. I left him by himself that night," she cries. "That was it. Everything became crystal clear in that moment—looking at his innocent, perfect little face, knowing that he wanted, *needed* his mama to clean up her act. I did. And I have never looked back."

I slam my sketchbook shut.

Holy crap. I drew her sleeping kid.

It's happening again.

• • •

My mom stands over me, over the toilet, watching me pee into a little plastic cup, making sure I don't dip into the toilet water and dilute whatever she suspects I have taken.

"Christ, Mom, I just got out of rehab this afternoon!"

She doesn't say anything.

I notice the dark circles around her eyes. The worry wrinkle between her eyebrows seems to be sinking deeper and deeper into her Italian olive skin, embedding itself into her forehead, cracking her face in two, and I feel compelled to say, to lie, "The meeting was good tonight, Mom. I may look for one with a younger crowd, though—they were all pretty old—but it was good."

"Finish up, Bea, I'm tired."

It doesn't matter what I say, the truth or a lie. She doesn't believe a word out of my mouth—nothing—ever since *that night* three months ago. Her eyes are set, staring at the prism-shaped cardboard stick that she has placed in the urine-filled cup. And she waits, sitting on the edge of the tub, picking at her paint-stained fingernails. One minute. Two. Three.

And as she waits, I see her relax bit by bit. The minutes tick by. She's noticing that none of the horizontal lines light up underneath the nefarious drug headings, and gradually the crevice between her eyes starts to fill in and her face solders back together again.

My urine is poured in the toilet and flushed, the cardboard stick and plastic cup tossed into the trash.

She sighs and hugs me, smelling of garlic and olive oil. "I'm glad you're home, Bea. Now get a good night's sleep. You have a big day tomorrow."

Shit. I'm trying not to think about that—starting my senior year, three and a half weeks late at a new school, the massive local public school, Packard High. Great. Just great.

3 months
1 day
12 hours

"Um, excuse me?" I ask the woman behind the cafeteria food counter with the purple hairnet and googly eyes. "You wouldn't happen to have anything vegetarian or anything, you know, healthy?" She looks at me as if I've asked for caviar, grunts, and points at something fluorescent green.

"Oh. Never mind. I guess I'll have that." I motion toward a pile of something red and beige. I think it's lasagna.

After paying for the plate of mystery food, I take in the vast and seemingly endless high school cafeteria. Packard High is a school with two thousand and something students. Damn, I don't think I've ever seen so many people in the same place all at once. Where the hell do I sit?

I pass table after table and see people's mouths moving up and down, chewing, probably whispering, "That's the rehab rat. She was kicked out of that fancy private school. What's with her hair?" Table after table—jocks, bros, stoners, pretty girls, nerds, loners—I can tell they all shun me like the herpes virus, like I have a red circle around me with a line drawn diagonally through it.

Ah . . . an empty table by the trash cans—just fine with me, and rather befitting, I'm sure, in the eyes of the teenaged masses.

I pile my wild, thick, Afro-slash-Italian-American, out-of-control dark hair on top of my head to prevent it from dipping into the sludge on the plate and fasten it with a couple of pens. It promptly falls out and into the faux lasagna. I sigh, lose my appetite, and write in my sketchbook:

I blame everything on my hair . . .
I do.

The pretty girl posse (they're at every school) pose at the table across from me. They, of course, have thick, luxurious, blow-dried hair and wear ridiculous cheerleading uniforms. I mean, everyone must know that they're cheerleaders—do they really have to advertise it? They giggle to themselves, dart their long-lashed eyes at me, and whisper.

And, as if on cue, I'm thrust back to Athena Day School for Girls—the school I was kicked out of—and hear the taunting, cruel words from elementary school. *Look at the Chia Pet! Beaver-head!*

I was born an artistic accident—sort of like one of Jackson Pollock's chaotic drip paintings—and was cursed with a combination of nappy Afro hair (from my dad) and thick, coarse Italian hair (from my mom). I've tried cutting it short—that's when I first heard the name "Chia Pet." Grew it shoulder length—hence Beaver-head. I tried *everything*. It consumed me, playing with my hair. After a while, I gave up and let it grow long, wild, and free.

And here I sit, alone at a table near the trash in a public high school cafeteria. I'm already behind in classes, already anticipating the attached label of "*Druggie* Chia Pet Beaver-head." Nightmare material, right?

What the hell. I can handle it.

I sit up a little straighter and "pen" my hair back up. After going through a rehab detox, this is nothing. They can't hurt me. Nothing, no one can.

Speaking of hair, some odd-looking dude with an Andy Warhol 'do and a camera around his neck is sashaying toward me, holding a paper-bagged lunch. Oh great. He's smiling and waving like he knows me, and now, oh shit, he's sitting down next to me.

"Bea? Beatrice Washington?"

"What? What did I do wrong?" I can't help the knee-jerk reaction.

"It's Chris. Chris Mayes." He purses his lips. "You don't remember me?"

I *so* want to be left alone. "I don't know. Should I?"

"Art camp, last winter break? I for sure remember you. You were like the best artist in the class. I sort of bleached my hair since then."

I squint my eyes and make a triangle with my hands, blocking out his hair. "Oh, right! Chris, of course. You were into photography."

He holds up his camera, points, and shoots. "Still am."

"Damn, you look nothing like yourself! You didn't bleach it, Chris—you fried it."

"Ha ha. Very funny."

"Yeah . . . I remember you—those skinny-ass jeans and the skinny, sexy ass inside them."

Chris plops his foot up on a chair, pointing at his colorful high-top Converse sneakers. "And these?"

"I can't believe it! You still have those?"

"Give me a break, Bea. Of course I do. They were hand-painted by a talented young artist—namely, you."

I finger the design—a red dragon, a few obscenities in purple, surrounded by gold and green swirls—painted when I was definitely high on something. "If I do say so myself, they are pretty damn cool. A little gay, but cool."

"Well, that would be me. Gay and cool." Chris puts his foot back on the ground. "You wouldn't believe the compliments. You still painting?"

"Ah, no. Been a little busy . . . rehabbing."

"Oh, of course . . . of course you have. I'm sorry, that was rude of me."

"No, no, Chris. No worries. I'm thrilled I actually know someone in this penitentiary. I had no idea you went to school here."

"It's unfortunate, but I do."

He looks down at my plate of food. "Holy Christ, Bea, what are you doing, eating that crap? Are you trying to poison yourself? Die young?" He tosses my tray into the garbage. "I'm going to have to lay down some rules for you. Rule number one: never, ever eat the food here. The woman who doles it out?"—he looks over at the googly-eyed lady—"The rumor is that she never graduated from high school, resents us all, carries a spray bottle of antifreeze in her pocket, and spritzes it on the food. Here, have half of my sandwich."

"Shit, that's gruesome. Okay, thanks, Chris." I happily take half of his peanut butter and jelly sandwich. "How did you find me, anyway? There's like a gazillion people here."

"Are you kidding? Your hair kind of stands out!"

"Um, look who's talking!"

Chris suddenly goes serious on me and plants his elbows on the table, resting his chin on his hands. "To tell you the truth, I was looking for you—heard through the gossip chain that you were coming somctime this week. They kicked you out, huh? Athena Day?"

I choke on a clump of peanut butter, and Chris hands me his water bottle. "Yeah. Athena Day School for Bitches—just got out of rehab yesterday."

"Wow, that's pretty heavy."

"Tell me about it. But I've been sober for three months—exactly three months, one day, and twelve hours." I look at the time on my phone. "And now fifteen minutes." I sigh.

Chris smiles, holding up his hand for a high five. "That's awesome!"

I question returning the slap.

"Uh . . . Bea? I'm waiting. You're not going to let me hang up here all alone, are you?"

"I'm not used to that, getting high-fived for being sober. Not from the people I hung out with, anyway."

"Well, poo on them. They're all at Bitch School, while you're here at Packrat High! Whoo hoo—high-five me already!"

The gazillion bangles on my wrist crash like cymbals as I slap his hand.

Chris likes the sound. "Nice."

"A nickel per bangle."

"I see you haven't stopped your hot retro look."

"Never, are you kidding me? Man, I missed my clothes—been wearing sweats for months."

"Did I happen to see vintage Doc Martens under the table?"

Now it's my turn to lift my foot. "Good eyes. Fifteen bucks, eBay."

"Get out of here."

I stand. "And this silk chiffon scarf I'm wearing around my waist? An original Yves Saint Laurent. I googled it—an old woman at a garage sale had no idea what she gave me for a dollar fifty!"

"Shut up! And that skirt . . . to die for."

"Fifties petticoat, in black!" I do a little curtsy for him and sit back down. "Trippy, don't you think? Thought it was perfect for my first day of school."

Chris beams. "You are the answer to my prayers, Beatrice Washington. I've been looking for a model."

"A model?"

"Yeah. I've been looking for someone to shoot—get my portfolio together, you know, for college. And all the girls around here are so . . . boring."

"College? Shit, that's the last thing I'm thinking about."

A cheerleader passes our table on the way to the trash and gives me the snooty once-over.

I give it a go and say, "Hi, my name is Bea. What's yours?"

She flips her flatironed hair over her shoulder, rolls her eyes, and rejoins her posse.

"How typical. They hate me already, and I haven't even done anything yet. It's my hair."

"Your hair is fierce, Bea! Rule number two: don't speak to the cheerleaders unless you are spoken to first."

"Excuse me?"

"They're harmless. Besides, they're in mourning."

"What do they have to be sad about?"

"Oh my god! You didn't hear about the rape?" Chris whispers.

"What rape? Who was raped?"

"Shhh!" Chris leans in closer to me. "Just the most

popular girl in our school, Willa Pressman. It happened a few weeks ago. Raped, left for dead. She's like the school's rock star, head cheerleader, elected homecoming queen."

"Is she here? With the other cheerleaders?"

Chris nods.

"Which one is she?"

"The blonde in the middle of the pack."

I look over at the cheerleader table. The girls hover over a frail-looking girl.

"Wow, she looks really zoned out. Is she okay?"

"I heard she was choked and beat up pretty bad—unconscious. A couple kids found her down by the creek."

"Shit, that's gruesome. Why in the hell is she here—back at school so soon?"

Chris shrugs. "I guess they think it's important for her to act 'normal' . . . whatever that means."

"They catch the guy?"

"Nope. He's still out there, and I guess she doesn't remember anything."

I shiver. "That's creepy. This is like the second attack in the past year."

"You mean that other girl, in the Arboretum last spring? But she was killed, and who knows if it was even the same guy."

"Yeah, who knows . . ." My mind wanders off, and I get caught in a stare.

"Um, Bea, you still with me?"

"Yeah." I shake off the stare. "It's just scary."

"I know, and everyone's wondering if Willa is going to show up to be crowned at homecoming Friday night—if she'll be able to handle it—you know, the spotlight, all the attention."

"You're not going, are you?"

Chris sighs. "I have to. I'm working the concession stand—service-learning hours."

"Oh yeah, I need those, too, like a million of them to graduate."

The bell rings.

Chris yells over the bell. "What class do you have next?"

I scramble in my bag for my schedule and laugh. "Art."

"Jinx. So do I. How cool is that? We're in the same class."

"Thank goodness, you can lead me there. This school is so huge, Chris—like a maze. I ended up in a shop class instead of algebra this morning."

Chris laughs. "Rule number three: stay away from the dudes in shop class. They all have woodies!"

"Chris! That's disgusting!"

"Depends on how you look at it." He giggles. "Don't worry, Bea. Stick with me. I'll help you master the Packrat maze and keep you celibate."

• • •

The desks are arranged in a circle, and it instantly reminds me of arts-and-crafts therapy at rehab. Jesus, was it lame. We'd have to sit in a circle and take turns sharing our "feelings" while gluing Popsicle sticks together, or something just as idiotic.

Chris and I take our seats, and the art teacher walks into the middle of the circle, tossing random objects on a lopsided table: a stapler, a pencil sharpener, a chipped coffee cup with lipstick stains. She takes hold of someone's ratty backpack and adds a ruler as the final touch.

"That's Mrs. Hogan," Chris whispers. "She is also the librarian and the school nurse. Budget cuts. She knows nothing about art. And don't get too close to her . . . her breath smells like rancid brussels sprouts!"

"Gross."

"Okay, everybody listen up." Mrs. Hogan stifles a yawn. "I'd like to welcome a new student in our class. Ah"—she reads from a piece of paper—"Miss Washington, Beatrice Washington."

Chris applauds the welcome, and I eyeball him. With my left hand under the desktop, I pull on a strategically placed hole in my black tights, ripping them, snagging the hole bigger, and wait for the whispers and finger-pointing.

But no one seems to take notice, no one gives a shit—they're all absorbed in their own worlds. A couple of kids text on their phones, a girl files her French-tipped nails, an obvious stoner naps, and my introduction thankfully fizzles away as Mrs. Hogan drones on. "Okay, class, today we're going to draw a still life. Notice how the light hits the objects, where the shadows fall." She makes herself comfortable behind her desk, delving into a gossip magazine.

I look at the chewed-up number-two pencil on the desk, sigh, pull a pen from my hair, and begin to draw the still life on the wrinkled, lined piece of paper in front of me.

I take on the fabric folds of the backpack's dark green canvas when she catches my eye—Willa, the cheerleader, the girl who was raped. She sits across from me, eye level above the planted backpack.

I study her milky white skin, the pale green and yellow bruises peeking out from the top of the cream-colored turtleneck underneath her cheerleading uniform. Her pink glossed lips are slack and open; her blue eyes, glassy and wet, are frozen in a heavy-lidded stare. She looks like a frightened, wounded deer.

Her pencil dangles from her right hand. Her head cocks slightly to the left as her gaze shifts away from the still life. It's as if she sees something—someone. I watch her breathe—even, steady, one, two, three. Exhale—one, two, three.

And in that moment, looking at Willa with my pen in my hand, a man's face explodes in my head, flashes in front of me. It shoots through my head and down my arm to my hand. Long nose; full, defined lips. He's staring at me, *in* me, *through* me. I see his sculpted high cheekbones, his chin—pointed, no beard, smooth complexion, his round wire-rim glasses, his dark brown eyes. I see them.

I draw them.

My hands tremble a little as I stare at Willa again. He's

there, in my head, maybe in her head? And now in front of me, on paper.

Oh my god! It's Marcus. Why did I draw Marcus?

I drop my pen. Chris leans over to pick it up and notices the sketch. "Who the hell is that?"

I startle at his question and turn over the paper, hiding the drawing. "It's nobody. Nothing."

My head throbs. I rub the back of my neck, take a deep breath, and look at Willa again. Her eyes blink open and closed, her lids droop—and she goes down, down on her desk, her blond mane covering her skinny arms.

I turn the paper over and peek at the sketch of the face. *This is so creepy. Why did I draw* him *when I looked at her? Why is this happening to me again?*

• • •

The school bell rings, and my first day at Packard High is over—and I managed to stay out of trouble. Whoo hoo.

Chris walks with me to my car—a kick-ass Volvo sedan junker. "So . . . what do you say we start off where we ended last winter?"

"Like the last half a year didn't happen? Would *love* to."

"So we're BFFs, right?"

"Were we ever best friends, Chris?"

He shrugs. "Sure we were . . . don't you remember?" He slugs me in the arm.

"Careful. This cardigan is at least fifty years old."

"Sorry." He pats my arm. "Hey, Bea, I was thinking . . . how about you help me out in the concession stand on homecoming? You need the hours, and I could use the company."

"Yeah, right. Me, at a homecoming? No way, Chris."

"Why not? You have something better to do?"

"AA." I roll my eyes.

"Come on, please?" Big smile.

A couple of bros pass us. They look our way, snickering, and I think I hear the words "queer-ass faggot" whispered.

Chris ignores them, but I know he heard. His cheeks redden, and his smile disappears.

"Hmm . . . you know, I do need those service-learning hours, Chris. I guess it's either that or tutoring little kids with lice or something gross like that after school." I shudder at the thought. "I hate kids."

"Oh my gosh, can you imagine picking nits out of your hair?" His smile returns. "Or you could choose to help file library books on the weekend with Mrs. Halitosis Hogan." He's laughing now.

"Okay—you one-upped me," I concede. "I'll join you on one condition."

"You name it."

"You can't look sexier than me, okay? Look at you in those jeans." I tease.

"Can't promise you that." He sways his hips. "Am I blushing?"

"I don't know, because the glaring white light from your hair is blinding me."

"Hey! I won't make fun of yours if you don't make fun of mine, Chia Pet."

I gasp. "How did you—"

"You told me a lot during art camp, Beaver-head. You were just too high to remember."

"Anything I should worry about?"

"Rule number four, Bea: what happens with Chris stays with Chris." He gives me a kiss on the cheek. "Remember to pack a lunch tomorrow."

"Will do, BFF." I slug him back.

• • •

I hook my right leg up and around the lowest branch and I climb. It's been a while, but I clamber up the stable, strong limbs, shredding my tights even more, until I settle in on one of the large, majestic boughs. It cradles me.

The tree is a massive sycamore on the front lawn of my house. She's been a trusty friend over the years. I have climbed her, watched her grow and fill out—her branches splayed in all directions, reaching out for me—even when I wasn't there for her. And I wasn't the last couple of years.

I light up a cigarette and blow the smoke away from the crinkly, triangular-lobed leaves. My thoughts are whirling around and around in my brain—trying to make sense of this drawing thing. I write in my sketchbook:

> I've always been able to draw—can draw anything I see in front of me, but now . . . what I draw seems like it's in other people's heads, and then it's suddenly in my head!

But Marcus? In that girl Willa's head? Why?

I pull the sketch out of my bag. It's his face—Marcus's face for sure. A pang hits my belly, hard.

> What the hell is happening to me?
> Am I nuts?

The first time it happened was at rehab. Everything was a blur—a horrible, nightmarish blur—the sweats, the insomnia, the jitters. I kept busy, tried to distract myself with drawing, always drawing. I found that my hands stopped twitching when I drew and kept me focused, a little more in control. I carried my sketchbook everywhere—I told them it was my bible—and it sort of was. They banned pens and pencils, thinking that we could use them to hurt ourselves (or others). So I hid my pens in my hair, holding it up. It was the first time I ever appreciated the density of my hair. I drew whenever they weren't looking—especially in my bedroom at night.

"Bea, stop it! Stop drawing me! I look like shit," Janine, my roommate at rehab, scolded me one night. "Oh god, I feel like shit."

She was shivering, going through alcohol withdrawal. And I was sketching her.

"You're a good subject, Janine, you don't move from your bed."

"Move? Are you kidding me? I wanna die, I feel so crappy. Just stop it, you bitch!"

I didn't listen to her. I had to draw. I had to draw the faded, floral spread that covered her body; her dirty blond hair tied loosely in a tangled ponytail. I studied the pattern of blemishes on her face, the shape of the Big Dipper, and *BAM!* It felt like an electrical shock. It zapped, exploded in front of me, filled my brain. A baby, a tiny baby—a fetus—curled up inside Janine. And I drew it—I had no choice but to draw it. It controlled me, owned my right hand.

The room started to spin.

Janine lit up a cigarette.

"I, um, I don't know if you should smoke, Janine."

"What the hell? Mind your own fucking business!"

"I could be wrong, but I . . . I think you may be . . ."

I passed out.

It was confirmed the next day with a routine urine test. Janine was eight weeks pregnant. She had a hunch her nausea wasn't just withdrawal and asked to switch roommates. She never spoke to me after that, but whenever I ran into her, she'd looked at me sideways, her left eye squinting.

That was the first time. But it kept happening.

I discovered my next roommate was still using. Her robe—that's what I saw, what I drew one night when I looked at her. But I didn't share that information—I wanted to check it out myself. Sure enough, when she was taking her shower the next morning, I found packets of cocaine sewn into the lining of her robe. I would have taken some—hell, yes I would have—if it weren't for the morning nurse bursting into our room to take my blood pressure.

That roommate didn't last long. Not long enough for me to score—not long enough for me to numb myself dumb, to stop the images. She was busted by lunch—didn't pass her urine test—and was thrown out of the facility.

I was honestly relieved when my pens were discovered and taken away by the director of the rehab. She did a pop-visit to my room one night. I was just doodling, but she yanked the pen out of my hand, seized my sketchbook, and leafed through it.

And then she saw it . . . a sketch of a man's menacing fist—poised—ready to punch something—someone. Her.

I had drawn it while studying her one day as she checked in another shaky, weepy addict. She tried to cover the bruises on her face with makeup, but that fist, that powerful, threatening fist set down in a drawing on a page in my sketchbook, exposed her. Exposed her painful secret.

"It's okay," I said. "I won't tell anyone if you don't want me to."

She swallowed—her hand touched her face—and she bore her eyes into me. "I don't know what you're talking about," her voiced cracked. "But you are not getting back your pens or this book, young lady!"

I was banned from drawing anything—even during arts-and-crafts therapy—and was never assigned another roommate. I was pissed but secretly happy for the punishment—relieved to have a break from the images.

I thought it was all about my withdrawing from the drugs, like a hallucination or something.

But now it's back, this strange power. Back with a tsunami force.

I can draw the truth out of people . . . literally.

I gaze down from the tree at my house, my home, the large, old brick Tudor on the edge of the University of Michigan campus. From the outside it looks like a comfortable family home, a home that you'd see on a sitcom—a family sitting around an oval dining room table, tying up a clichéd, episodic mishap in a neat and tidy half hour. But it's far from that, for sure.

I look through the smudged windows of my dining room—we don't have a housekeeper, and the last thing my mom would think of doing is wash a window. No, the interior of my house doesn't much resemble a sitcom set. The dining room table is covered with a drop cloth instead of a white linen tablecloth, and my mom's painting paraphernalia takes the place of the baked chicken and mashed potatoes. She specializes in painting murals in people's homes—something my dad scoffs at (being the art snob that he is)—and practices on the walls of our house. Puppy dogs, balloons, kids' names I don't recognize line the walls.

I can see my mom through the window. Annabelle is her name—or Bella, as my dad likes to call her—and she's a fiery Italian hothead. She's sitting—painting, of course.

My mom and dad met at art school in Chicago—both talented young artists. But my dad eventually gave up drawing and painting for some reason and continued in academics. Then they had me, and my mom put her studies on hold. But Dad barreled through school, got his PhD, was appointed the art chair at the University of Michigan, and moved Mom and me to Ann Arbor. She never got her degree, but she continues to paint daily—puppy dogs and flowers. "It helps me stay sober," she says.

Yes, my mom passed that powerful gene on to me.

Do I dare try it on her? Draw what's on my mom's mind?

She's wearing one of my dad's large white oxford shirts. (He hates it when she wears them because of paint stains, and that's exactly why she does.) The sleeves are rolled up, revealing her long, thin, olive arms holding a paintbrush.

And it happens again, but it's more like pressure in my head this time—something trying to get through to me. And it does. I see it: a glass of wine. I draw a crystal goblet filled to the brim with dark, blood red wine. *Mom is thinking about a glass of red wine!*

Shit . . . she's been sober for over ten years
and she still thinks of drinking?
I'm doomed.

The sun is beginning to set, and the temperature has dropped a couple degrees. I see that my mom is checking the time on her watch, I'm sure a little worried about where I am. She picks up her cell phone and dials—my number, I know it.

I hide my cigarette behind my back just as my phone rings (set to David Bowie's "Rebel Rebel"). "Hi, Mom."

"Where are you?" She sounds on edge.

"Out here—look out the window. I'm up in the tree."

My mom turns toward the window.

I wave.

"Beatrice Francesca Washington! What are you doing up there? You haven't been up there in years. Don't you think you're a little old to be climbing a tree?"

"How old do people get before they stop climbing trees?"

"Don't sass me, Bea."

"You want to join me, Mom?"

"Why would I want to do that?"

"I don't know . . . is there anything you want to talk about?"

"No. Why?"

"No reason."

"Bea, you're acting odd. Are you having a cigarette? Is that what you're doing? You know I don't like that habit you picked up at rehab. Come down here *right now*!"

I spit on my fingers and put out my cigarette, stick the butt in the pack. My thoughts have drifted back to the sketch of Marcus. *I have to go see him, have to find out why he's on that girl Willa's mind.*

"Hey, Mom, would you mind if I hit a meeting after dinner? I feel like I need to," I lie.

There's no way Mom will say no to that request.

3 months
1 day
19.5 hours

He lives in a frat house on the University of Michigan campus with a bunch of Wolverine jocks. Marcus himself is not a jock—far from it—but he supplies them (and others) with a steady flow of stimulants, downers—whatever they need to keep up with their classes and the dreaded stopwatch. He helps anorexic sorority chicks with unwanted weight gain; athletes with home runs and touchdowns; and the run-of-the-mill drug addicts with their addictions.

My parents think I'm at a meeting, so I have an hour and a half before I have to be home, before they wig out.

I pull up to the dark brick fraternity house, and as usual, a rowdy party is in full swing.

Breathe . . . just breathe, Bea.

I step out of my car. Someone stumbles off the front porch; a couple is having audible sex in the second-floor Juliet balcony. I know the setting well, too well—and I know where to go, where to find Marcus. I was a regular fixture here for a while.

Marcus, ironically, is a bookish type and a boyfriend my parents approved of—even though he was two years older than me and my drug dealer. They didn't know that side of Marcus, and he's brilliant at winning people over. He said "thank you" and "please," put his napkin on his lap, and held the door open for my mom. He's a charmer and comes from a proper Jewish family in Philadelphia. His family believes in him, believes that he is pursuing a career in premed pharmaceuticals. And that is exactly what Marcus does. Provide pharmaceuticals.

No one would ever suspect the nice Jewish boy from Philadelphia of being a campus drug dealer. Never.

I wind my way up the crowded, dark wooden staircase and juke the jocks. My ass is pinched by a drunken douche bag. He recognizes me but has a hard time getting his wet, sloppy mouth and brain around my name, as simple as it is. And if he did talk to me? His paranoid, skinny girlfriend would most certainly throw him over the top of the oak banister. Three floors down. *Splat.*

I continue up toward the attic. A steep, narrow staircase leads me to the dreaded dormered door. It's hobbitlike, silent, and serene.

I know the knock. Once. Wait. Kick low. Wait. And cough twice.

My stomach starts warming up like coils in a toaster oven, and a surge of electrified heat crawls through my body.

A craving is what it is.

My mind tells me to turn away now and run—run fast and high-jump over the flights of stairs, over all the slop and muck that I've avoided for three months now.

But my body battles my mind. My palms itch, my mouth is dry, and I want relief, I *need* relief, and I know that two inches of an oak door separate *me* from *it*.

And that door opens.

"Bea!" Marcus smiles and takes me in his arms. He buries his face in my hair and whispers, his mouth brushing the lobe of my ear, "I knew you'd be back, my little bumble Bea." He kisses my neck. "You smell the same . . . like honey."

I start to melt.

He takes a step back and gestures for me to enter his room. "Come on in."

I do, and he closes the door.

A Bach concerto plays through high-end Bose speakers. Textbooks cover his desk, lit by an amber-glassed library lamp. Jack Kerouac's *On the Road* sits open on his bed.

Marcus looks deep into my eyes. "How are you? I tried calling you, over and over—you never answered."

"Yeah, they took my phone away, my parents. Cut me off from all my friends and from you. I ended up in rehab for three months. Did you know that, Marcus?"

He strokes my cheek with his callous-free palm and nods. "I did. Oh, babe. I'm so sorry. You need anything . . . to take the edge off?"

"No, no, Marcus, I didn't come for that." I pull away. "But I'll take a bottle of water, if you have one."

"Sure, of course." He pulls one out of a minifridge.

Whistler, a gray Maine coon cat the size of a medium-sized dog, comes running over, purring—twisting around my legs.

"Whistler." I bend down, drop my purse to the floor, and pick up my furry friend. "How have you been?" I scratch under his chin.

Marcus unlocks a tall antique cabinet. I know the cabinet well, and I know what's in it. He pushes aside a few leather-bound books, peruses the stash, and takes out a plastic bottle filled with tiny pink pills.

"Marcus, no. Please, I didn't come for that. I told you. Please."

He doesn't seem to hear me, removes Whistler from my arms, placing him on his bed, and takes my sweaty hand in his, dropping two pills onto my palm.

"You'll feel better, I promise." He lifts my chin with his hand. "I'm so happy you're here, Bea."

And I am suddenly there. Back. Back in the dark alleys of my life . . .

• • •

It was last April, right after my seventeenth birthday, and I was running with Marcus in the Arboretum, hand in hand through a field of hip-high alfalfa and rye grass. We were high out of our minds, giggling and leaping over downed hickory trees, somersaulting on the grass until we found a hidden gully at the base of a wooden bridge that arched over a trickling spring.

"Heaven!" Marcus sang out. "This is it . . . we found heaven!"

He pulled me down on the grass and rolled over on top of me. "You're so beautiful, Bea. Your hair, oh your hair." He studied it, seemed mesmerized by it. "And your body, your skin—so beautiful, like a frothy caramel cappuccino." He kissed my neck. His tongue flickered in my ear. "So sweet," he purred, kissing my lips. His hands moved under my cropped madras top, and he caressed my bare belly. He fingered the hand-painted ivy on the thighs of my jeans, and slowly, ever so slowly, started unzipping them.

"Marcus, we should stop—"

But he covered my mouth with his hand and quoted Jack Kerouac: "'A pain stabbed my heart, as it did every time I saw a girl I loved who was going the opposite direction in this too-big world.'"

I dissolved into the words even though I had no idea what they meant. We were oblivious of time, oblivious of the sudden rainstorm. And, with our sweaty bodies entwined, we fell into a deep, thick-as-molasses sleep.

"Help. Help me," I heard. "Help, please . . ."

A voice. A weak, tortured voice breaking through the

heavy fog in my head. A voice of a girl. "Could it be me?" I asked myself in my stupor. "Am I calling for help? Why would I be calling for help?"

I rolled over to my side and tried to make out where the voice was coming from.

"Marcus, I think someone needs help," I slurred. But I didn't see him, couldn't find him. He wasn't by me anymore. "Marcus? Marcus, where are you?"

I heard faint, hoarse coughs, a slight moan, I thought, over beyond the bridge, down toward the orchid conservatory, and I tried to crawl, in slow motion, it seemed, to the voice. I managed to drag my heavy-limbed, hallucinating body two feet, then fell back into the damp, sleepy grass, and the voice stopped—dead.

I awoke at dusk with my phone ringing. Unread text messages buzzed, disturbing the peaceful surroundings. Sirens wailed in the not-so-far distance.

"Turn that thing off." Marcus was back, lying next to me.

My phone buzzed again. "Shit. What's going on, anyway?"

I squinted my eyes and read the text from my mom.

bea where r u??? heard on news theres been a murder. they found a body. a young girl in the arboretum! please call me. im scared. please. where r u?!!!?

"Marcus. Marcus, wake up." I shook him. I shook him hard.

"Easy, easy. What's going on?" he grumbled.

"Someone was killed here today—here at the Arb. A girl."

And I remembered. Her voice rushed back to me, her pleading words. "I heard her cry for help. I thought I was dreaming. And I couldn't find you, Marcus."

"Shit. Are the cops here?"

"I could have helped her. She was alive. She was. She can't be dead. I heard her."

"You were hallucinating—tripping on the 'shrooms, Bea."

"You think that was it? You heard things, too? Voices?"

"We gotta get out of here, fast."

We scrambled, throwing on our wet clothes as we heard approaching walkie-talkie voices and dogs panting and barking.

"Shit. Run," Marcus ordered.

"But we didn't do anything."

"I'm holding, Bea! I have a drop scheduled today."

We sprinted through the knee-high alfalfa grass again, but this time it was wet and muddy, and I tripped over rotten, felled trees. Burrs tangled in my hair.

We stopped at a two-lane road, saw police cars approaching. Marcus pushed me down into a ditch of wet leaves and mud, and I fell on a jagged rock. My jeans ripped, and I scraped my knee, drawing blood.

"Bea, come on, get up!" Marcus pulled me across the road and onto a side street to his parked car. I brushed the dirt off my top and torn jeans and dabbed a used tissue on my bleeding knee.

Marcus started his car and sped off.

• • •

I read every report of her rape and murder in the days and weeks that followed. Her name was Veronica, and she was an eighteen-year-old senior at a high school in Ypsilanti. Her arms and legs were tied. She was blindfolded, and wet leaves covered her face. A black garbage bag was wrapped around her legs. The only thing exposed was her bruised and battered torso. They said she was strangled after she was beaten and raped. And they had no leads, no answers—nothing.

I never came forward, never had the guts to tell anyone that I thought I was there when she was still alive, still fighting for her life—that I thought I had heard her—and if I did, if it was her voice, I could have saved her. But I was too messed up to help. And too ashamed to admit it. So I got messed up even more after that.

But her voice, calling for help, never left me. No drug, nothing I took, could erase it from my head.

And now he may have struck again, with Willa.

I look at Marcus, present time, hand him back the pills, throw my shoulders back, and sip the water. "No thanks, Marcus. I can't."

"Okay. I won't force you." He drops them into a tiny envelope and backs away, trips on my purse, swears, and places my bag on his desk.

"Marcus, the reason I came here was to ask you about a girl named Willa . . . Willa Pressman."

He swings around, facing me. "Why?"

"Do you . . . know her?"

He laughs. "You came here to ask me if I know the strung-out chick who was raped?"

"Strung out? What are you talking about, Marcus? She's like a goddess to everyone at that school."

"Yeah, that may be, but she's a strung-out goddess."

"Seriously? She uses?" I sit down on his desk chair, stunned.

"Oh, come on, an addict can recognize another a mile away. Don't act so surprised. How do you know her, anyway?"

"I just met her today. I go to her school now."

"Ah, Packard High, know it well. A frequent stop for me. Those kids there keep me busy."

"So you supply her?"

He laughs. "Ah, I think a few of us do—her appetite is insatiable."

"Wow. Really. Well, I heard her bring your name up in the lunchroom, and I wondered—"

Marcus panics. "She's not, like, talking shit about me, ratting me out, is she?"

"No, no. It's not like that. I was sort of surprised she knew you." I scramble. "And it got me wondering about you—how you're doing."

He kneels, eye level with me, rolls my chair closer to him. "I'm doing just fine . . . especially now. I've missed you, baby. I'm glad you came." He leans in and kisses me, and I taste him, succumb to his sweet, warm mouth—and realize it wasn't just his drugs I was addicted to.

The words fly out of my mouth before I can think. "Oh, Marcus, I've missed you, too . . . so much."

He pulls me up off the chair and backs us onto his bed. Whistler hisses as he is forced off the pillow. Marcus, lying above me, starts to unbutton my cardigan, kissing the skin underneath.

The door suddenly slams wide open, and Aggie stands above us. Agatha Rand, my ex-best friend from Athena Day.

"Aggie!" Marcus sits up.

She can barely stand. Her long, dark auburn hair falls over half of her face. Mascara is smudged under her eyes. She stumbles on her heels as she walks over to the bed and sits down by us. Her tight black dress scootches up, revealing her firm, spray-tanned thighs.

I stand. "What are you doing here, Aggie? What's she doing here?" I ask Marcus. "Are you two . . . oh my god, while I was in rehab? You two hooked up?"

Marcus looks irritated at Aggie. "Of course not, Bea. She's just a friend."

"Holy shit." Aggie starts laughing. She crumples down onto the pillow, smiles, and says, "Oh my god, this shit, Marcus, this shit you gave me, it's like—oh my god, come here and gimme a hug. Oh, wow . . . Beeeeea . . . isthatyou? Shit I thi' I gonna be—" And she vomits over the side of the bed.

"Holy crap!" Marcus rushes to the bathroom for a towel.

Whistler leaps up onto the windowsill, his fur fluffed.

I button my sweater and look down at Aggie, now sleeping soundly, looking very comfortable in Marcus's bed. Her breath is calm and relaxed through her drooling, slack jaw. Chunks of barf cling to her auburn curls. Her left breast falls out of the top of her dress.

Is that what I looked like? Was that me?

Marcus cleans the puke off the floor. "Bea . . . she just comes to me for shit, that's all."

I grab my purse. "Fuck you. I have to get out of here."

• • •

I make it to the last fifteen minutes at St. Anne's so the mediator can sign my card and prove to my parents that I was there, at the meeting. I barge in, out of breath, make up a crazy story about a flat tire and having to walk miles to a gas station to get help.

The group looks at me, no expression on their faces, no "yeah, right, your dog ate your homework" kind of look. They seem to accept the lie. The Hawaiian-shirt guy signs the card, no problem. "We look forward to seeing you again, Bea."

Unreal.

I make it home by curfew.

3 months 3 days 12 hours

"This is nice, Chris." I breathe in the crisp, clean autumn air as we eat our paper-bagged lunches on the bleachers above the football field. Chris snaps photos of the colorful maples across the stadium.

"Look at the beautiful colors—the orange blanket of leaves," Chris says, looking through the lens.

"Pretty, aren't they?" But I'm not looking at the maples—I'm looking at Chris, how happy he is—how content he is with a simple tree. I sketch, but it isn't the tree I draw.

Suddenly and rudely, the blanket of leaves is trampled and crushed by the incoming cleats of the football players.

I close my sketchbook. "Shit, it was so peaceful. Why do they have to practice during lunch?"

"The homecoming game. It's Friday, remember?" He puts his camera cap on.

I roll my eyes. "Right. Can't wait."

Chris elbows me. "Hey, it's our first date. I happen to be looking forward to it."

I offer him a celery stick. "You know . . . I saw a couple old friends the other night."

Chris looks at me with concern. "Uh-oh. You stayed out of trouble?"

"Yeah, yeah, I did, thank goodness. But it got me thinking."

Chris dips the celery into the peanut butter on his sandwich. "About what?"

"That maybe they weren't friends after all. And I don't know . . . it makes me sad. I feel like a fool."

Chris puts his arm around me. "Well, now you have me."

I smile. "I do, don't I?"

"You do."

"Hey, Chris, you want to go shopping with me after school?"

"Really? Wow, could I?"

"I was planning on going to my favorite thrift store. Maybe we could find something kickass to wear Friday night?"

"I'm in. Thanks."

The football players begin to run up the bleacher stairs in formation, two at a time, chanting "hut hut" with each step.

Chris's backpack is in the way of Jersey #9, a hulking fullback, and before Chris can move it, the jerk kicks, slamming the pack into Chris's leg. "Get your fucking bag outta the way, you limp-wrist homo!"

"What the . . . ?" I jump up, ready to chase after the asshole, ready to take the stairs three at a time and punch his lights out, when Chris holds me back.

"Rule number five, Bea: don't try to take a football player down."

"Did you hear what he called you?"

"Leave it alone. It doesn't matter. It's just a name." Chris takes an apple out of his lunch bag and starts munching away like it's no big deal.

"I can't believe that doesn't bother you! You shouldn't let people get away with it."

"Stick and stones may break your bones, but names will never hurt you," Chris singsongs.

"Are you kidding me?"

He laughs. "It's okay, Bea, don't stress."

"It's not okay! Name-calling is worse than a broken bone—it can't be set in a cast and healed in six weeks. I would know. It hurts!"

"Jesus"—he laughs at my fury—"you'd think you were the one called a homo."

"Yeah, well, you're my friend. And I guess I'm a little sensitive about bullying," I growl. "Give me your apple."

"What for?"

"Just give it to me." I snatch the apple from his hands, aim, and throw it at Jersey #9. The fruit splatters on the back of his clean white jersey.

Chris jumps up, slings his backpack over his shoulder.

"You shouldn't have done that. He's going to think I did it. I'm getting out of here." He starts running up the bleachers.

I follow him. "Oh, come on . . . he didn't even feel it. It bounced right off of his steroidal shoulders."

"Girls and boys!" a voice blasts through the loudspeakers.

"Holy crap!" I startle. "Who was that?"

Chris turns, looks to the stadium speakers. "That would be the great Oz, our principal Mr. Nathanson."

"Please come to the auditorium immediately!"

"Do you think he saw me throw the apple? Am I in trouble?"

Chris laughs and puts an arm around me. "No, he's not Big Brother. I'm sure he's just calling an impromptu pep rally."

"Oh goodie—a pep rally!" I roll my eyes. "Ra, ra, sis boom bah!"

• • •

The whole student body, all couple thousand of us, is corralled into a squeaky-clean, state-of-the art, gigantic gymnasium. I look up, marveling, taking in the dozens and dozens of giant felt banners hanging high above us on the towering walls, boasting of championships in soccer, baseball, basketball, hockey—every sport imaginable. I nudge Chris. "I guess there are no budget cuts happening in the sports program, huh?"

Chris finds us seats on the edge of one of the lacquered maple risers.

The sweaty football players are the last to enter and are slouching by the locker room doors, adjusting their cups and shoulder pads.

At their appearance, a couple of cheerleaders run into the middle of the floor and begin to flip over each other like golden retriever puppies. They start an impromptu cheer. "PACK HIGH, PACK HIGH, PACK HIGH!!!"

"Excuse me, ladies!" a voice booms over the loudspeaker. This time, I see where it comes from—a portly, balding man in glasses, standing at a microphone underneath one of the basketball hoops.

"I take it that's the great Oz?" I ask Chris.

He nods.

"Please, please, girls, please take your seats. This is not a pep rally. I didn't call you in for that."

The stands roar with laughter—especially the football players—and I almost feel sorry for the two girls as they leave the floor with their tails between their legs.

"Thank you, girls and boys, for joining me. I called you here to tell you some rather disturbing news. A girl has gone missing. She is, um, from a neighboring high school. That's all we know."

A collective inhale—two thousand and something audible gasps suck the air out of the gym.

"Holy shit," Chris and I say together.

"Calm down, calm down. We don't know yet if foul play is involved," the principal continues.

The buzzing starts, the audible whispers. "Where's Willa?" "Who was she?" "Where did it happen?"

"Don't worry about Miss Pressman, we already sent her home," the principal says. "But we have no idea if this has anything to do with, well, what happened to her. So, on a happier note, after great deliberation, we have decided to go ahead with the homecoming game Friday night."

Big cheer. The cheerleaders, apparently over their shame, perform cartwheels across the squeaky floor.

"Are you kidding me?" I ask Chris. "Why would they go ahead with a stupid football game? A girl is missing. A rapist is loose. This is crazy!"

The principal continues. "We feel you all deserve a night of levity, with everything that's happened. The police will have a heavy presence, but please, please be extra cautious. Stay close to one another. Stick with a buddy."

Chris puts his arm around me and squeezes. "Will you be my buddy? I won't lie—I'm spooked."

"Of course." I pat his hand.

"And, boys and girls, if you need to talk, you all know that we have a school counselor on hand." The principal gestures toward Mrs. Hogan, the art teacher/librarian/nurse/counselor with the bad breath. She waves.

Groans from the stands.

"Okay, okay, now, I believe the bell will ring in—"

And it does, drowning out Principal Nathanson's parting words.

Chris looks at me. "I wonder who she is, the poor girl."

• • •

I rifle through a rack of vintage coats at the thrift shop and take a big sniff. "Chris, don't you love the smell? Every piece of clothing here has a history, a story."

Chris holds up a pair of whacked-out bell-bottoms. Erect penises are embroidered on the back pockets. "I wonder what his story was." He laughs.

I raise an eyebrow. "I bet you would."

Chris throws the pants at me. "Bitch."

"Ewww! I don't want them to touch me!" I hurl them back at him. "Oh, wow, look at this." I pull a paisley velvet coat off a hanger. Great colors: gold and greens. Size six. "This is awesome." I try it on and swirl around in front of a mirror. "It fits perfectly, doesn't it, Chris? It's missing a couple buttons, but it's only twenty-five bucks."

Suddenly the store is rocked with blaring, screaming sirens. Chris and I run to the front window and see police cars, a couple of fire trucks, and an ambulance race by.

Leila, the owner of the shop, joins us. "Wow. I wonder what happened?"

"It's probably about that girl. The girl who's missing." Chris chews his fingernails.

"What girl?" Leila asks.

"Someone from around here," I say. "I bet she just ran

away or something—got pissed at her parents. Believe me, I've thought about running away—more than once, for sure."

"Well, I'm glad you didn't, Bea. I'm very happy for your business." Leila smiles.

"Hey, Bea? Let's get out of here. I want to go home."

"You wuss."

"I am not."

"Okay, fine. I have to hit a meeting anyway." I place the paisley coat on the counter. "I'll buy this, Leila. Chris? Did you pick out something?"

"Well, it's between the penis pants and the pimp hat I found in the back. What do you think?" He holds up the pants and a wide-brimmed zebra print fedora.

I laugh at my new best—and only—friend. "Okay, when it comes to shopping, *I'm* setting some rules. Rule number one: never buy anything that has a penis embroidered on it. Rule number two: never, *ever* put a hat on your head that you haven't cleaned first. Rule number three—well, this is a question, not a rule—do you *like* being bullied, girlfriend?"

3 months
5 days
19 hours

Big date with Chris tonight!
Homecoming . . . working a concession stand.
Who woulda thunk?

After sewing buttons on my new coat and spending an hour scrounging around in my closet, changing from one outfit to another, I decide on crushed velvet, skintight pants topped with a black cashmere sweater. I'm allergic to wool, but I figure it's going to be a little nippy, and the coat isn't that warm. I finish off my look with my over-the-knee, black, stiletto-heeled "don't fuck with me" boots—for Chris's sake, since I'm his designated buddy tonight.

"Supper!" my mom calls up the stairs.

Oh shit . . . family dinner night!

Dinner together was never a priority with my family. We all fended for ourselves, and it was just fine that way, if you ask me. This "dinner" thing is something new that my parents insist on ever since . . . well, ever since that night.

I tromp down the stairs to the kitchen in protest. But they are, as usual, in the middle of an argument and don't even notice. Mom is standing at the stove, sautéing something in a pan. Cooking is not her talent, but whatever's in the pan has plenty of garlic in it.

"What do you *mean* you can't grab some spray paint from the supply room? You're the chair, Richard!"

"It isn't right, Bella. It's like stealing."

"Oh, give me a break. There has to be some perk to your job. It certainly isn't your salary."

I've heard this argument for years. It doesn't faze me much. Mom is trying to score free art supplies, and she usually succeeds, but Dad has to go through the motions of arguing about it—makes him feel better.

I clear my throat, announcing that I'm dutifully here, ready to eat, bond, hold hands, and sing "Kumbaya," which will undoubtedly cure me of all my demons.

My mom checks me out, looking me up and down. Here comes the criticism. I can smell it; it's as strong as the garlic she's cooking. She can't help herself.

"You're wearing *that*?"

"What's wrong with it?"

"Yeah, what's wrong with what she's wearing? It doesn't look used, like most of her clothes. No holes. It's fine with me," Dad says.

"She happens to be allergic to wool, and that sweater is cashmere."

I sigh as they talk about me as if I'm not in the room with them.

"Well, she'd better not come to me when she breaks out in hives. And those boots—the heels are rather high. She's going to trip in the bleachers and fall flat on her face."

"She told me she's working in the concession stand," Dad says. "She looks fine, Bella, leave her alone. Choose your battles."

I hang my coat on the back of my chair and sit.

"Where did you get that coat?"

"It was only twenty-five dollars at the thrift store, Mom."

Mom looks at Dad.

"Take it out of my allowance. I don't care."

Dad sits back in his chair. "Your mother and I think you should look for a job—earn your spending money."

"A job? Are you kidding me? With all the studying I have to do to catch up?"

"You're a bright girl, Bea. I don't think you'll have a hard time catching up—especially at *that* school." Dad sighs.

"You know, I'm painting a mural at a preschool—"

"Don't you dare go there. No way!" I say.

"It's close, part-time—a couple of hours after school watching the kids."

"Mom, I hate kids!"

"But you *love* clothes, don't you?" she counters.

Damn. She trumped me.

"They're expecting you Monday afternoon. You should wear something . . . practical."

Ping. My cell phone buzzes in my bag—a text from Chris.

CHRIS: where r u?
ME: dinner b there asap
CHRIS: wtf? u were supposed to b here now
ME: ik chill omw

"No texting at the table, Bea, you know the rules." Dad wipes his mouth with his napkin.

What a charade. There are no rules—never have been during dinner. "It's Chris, Dad."

"Chris, your date?"

"Yeah." I laugh to myself. "My date."

My mom arches a brow. "And you'll be with him all evening?"

"Of course."

"It's great that you made a friend already," Dad says.

"It'd be nice to meet him. Have him over for one of our dinners," Mom suggests.

Oh god, please, no! "Chris is like super busy, Mom. He's in a lot of clubs at school."

"How nice for him. Maybe you could join one?" Mom asks.

"But I wouldn't be able to . . . you know, if I have to work after school." *Touché*.

She blinks, changes the subject. "You'll be coming home right after the game?"

"I may hit a meeting, but I'll let you know."

My parents look at each other. One thing they can agree on: worrying about me.

"Call us every hour and let us know where you are," Dad says.

"And we'll have you pee in the cup tonight," Mom adds.

I glare at my parents. "Are you serious? When is that going to end? Huh? When are you going to trust me again? Jesus."

"There's a crazy person out there, Bea," my dad says, raising his voice. "A girl was raped at your school, and another one is missing." He takes a deep breath. "We just want to make sure you're safe."

"You don't trust me, admit it."

But then again, why should they?

• • •

That night—last July Fourth, Dad drove me to my best friend Agatha's house because my car was in the shop. I'd backed into our mailbox the week before. (Yes, I was high.)

With a peck on the cheek, I told my dad two lies in one sentence. "We're going to watch the fireworks in the park, and yes, her parents are home, Dad."

"You sure?" He placed his hand on top of mine.

"Daaad! Yes, I'm sure. Stop worrying so much! You and Mom are like the strictest parents. None of my friends get the third degree and have to check in as much as I do. Chill."

He talked through tented fingers at his lips. "I respect your feelings, and I will take them under consideration. What concerns me—and I'll be honest with you—your mother thought you were acting funny the other day when you backed your car into the mailbox. You aren't experimenting with illegal substances . . . drugs, are you?"

I busted out with a well-rehearsed laugh. "Oh, give me a break. Drugs? I'm not stupid. And Mom? She thinks everyone acts funny—it's the Italian paranoid blood in her. She reads into things all the time, you know that."

"That she does." He smiled to himself. Successful deflection on my part. "Okay, well, I'm glad we had this little talk. Be safe—and stay in touch. Keep your phone on. I love you."

"Mwaa!" I air-kissed my father, walked through the wrought-iron gates and up the slick stoned driveway to Aggie's parentless house.

The Rands are two hotshot lawyers, and they're never home. That night they were at a wedding in Grosse Pointe—a weekend excursion—and, as always, left their housekeeper, Maria, to look after Agatha.

I liked Maria. I don't know . . . she and I had a connection. Maybe it was the yummy guacamole she made for me. Maybe it was her hotheadedness—growing up with Italian expletives, I understood her Spanish barbs and interjections, usually directed at Agatha's behavior. "*Que dios te bendiga*, Agatha!"

This was our plan: after Maria went to bed, we would slip out the window, hop into Marcus's car, and go to a rave at a Detroit club that Aggie had RSVP'd to online the week before.

Maria answered the door and gave me a hug, and I ran up the stairs to Aggie's bedroom.

"Hey," Agatha said, snorting a line of coke.

"Hey." I unzipped my long, baggy U of M sweatshirt, revealing a striped yellow and black halter top over a micro-miniskirt. I took a pair of platform sandals out of my backpack and strapped them on. "Do I look bitchin', or what?" I twirled in front of her full-length mirror.

Aggie looked at me wild-eyed and started to laugh, falling on her bed. "You look like a stupid bee in that top! A frigging bumble bee!"

It was obvious that she was already totally tweaked, and I suddenly had second thoughts about my outfit—and the night. "You know, I was thinking. Maybe we should stay local. I've heard crazy, scary stories about these raves. You sure we should go?"

Aggie stopped laughing and shot me a hard, cold look. "Chill, Bea. Sometimes you're such a downer."

Nine o'clock arrived. Maria was in her bedroom with the door closed, watching reruns of old soap operas.

Ping.

MARCUS: down the block. car running

We slipped out of Aggie's window and down the ivy-covered trellis on the back side of her house—no problem, even with the platform sandals, as we had accomplished the trek many times. We giggled down the street, high-fiving about our deception, and hopped into Marcus's silver Prius. He had a lit joint waiting for us (and a tongue-filled kiss for me), and we took off into the night.

The club was packed, hopping with frenetic, shit-faced energy. Trance DJs flooded the club with pulsating electronic dance music. Our sweaty bodies, waving glow sticks, moved in sync with the mind-blowing, deafening, throbbing beat under the flashing strobe lights.

I moved in slow motion, it seemed, with my eyes closed—around and around in circles—and lost track of my friends. The room started to spin, and I got nauseated. I looked for Aggie. I looked for Marcus. I called out their names, but with the music blasting, I couldn't even hear my own voice.

And then I saw them, Marcus and Aggie, through my swollen, squinty eyes. They were leaning on a railing across the room, touching each other. He played with her hair, twisted it around and around in his fingers. They started to laugh, and I thought they were pointing at me—at my clothes—looking like a bee. I saw them walking off together, holding hands.

Some guy asked me if I was okay and handed me a drink. I thanked him and stumbled to the john. "Aggie. You there?" I slurred. I looked for them behind the club. I think I tried to text them, but my fingers felt like fat toes.

I couldn't find them anywhere. So I decided to drink the drink. I don't know if there was anything else in it—like something more than booze—but I got shit-faced wasted after that. I ingested, snorted, and inhaled, and in my inebriated stupor I took off my stupid halter top, threw it in the air, and was lifted up and passed around topless, like a tray of hors d'oeuvres. I blacked out and was apparently dropped.

I never felt my rib crack.

Aggie somehow got safely home and into her bed. She played dumb and innocent with her parents and the teachers at school, telling them all that I was the druggie; and that I tried to force her to go to the rave; and that when she said no, I snuck out of her window while she was sleeping; and that she never wanted to have anything to do with me again.

Fuck her. But since the library at Athena Day was named the Rand Library, I guess fuck *me*, right?

Regardless, someone called 9-1-1. I was rushed to the emergency room as an overdosed, topless, crazy-haired Jane Doe.

I woke up in a hospital bed. My mom was crying over me, blubbering, her dark, mascara-tinged tears dripping onto my crisp white pillow as she prayed on a rosary, making the sign of the cross with her long, blue-veined hands. My dad was pacing, swearing, and punching the walls like a gang member from Detroit.

"Hi," I uttered.

"Bea!" They shouted in unison. "Beatrice!"

And the first thing I thought of was how much pain I was in and that I could possibly manipulate them in *their* pain. "Um, Mom, Dad? Do you think they could, um, give me something? Like a painkiller? OxyContin? Maybe I should give Marcus a call . . . where's my phone?"

I manipulated myself right into rehab.

• • •

I look at my parents at the kitchen table and bite into a piece of cold, waxy polenta. It tastes like guilt, if guilt had a taste. "Fine, whatever. You can test me, and I'll call you every hour. You're so uptight."

Everyone swallows.

Dad puts his fork down on the table like a punctuation mark. "I think this is terrific—nice that we're having dinner together again. I like this." He doesn't.

Another ping on my cell—I'm sure from Chris, wigging out.

Mom darts her dark eyes at me. I don't dare answer it.

"So," my dad says, looking for something to talk about, "you should start on your college applications, what do you think?"

"Oh, for chrissake, she just got out of rehab," Mom cuts in.

"I know that. But it's time to look ahead to the future.

In fact, I've scheduled a tour for Bea at the university," he announces.

"You what?" Mom asks, more surprised than me.

"I don't know, Dad. I don't know if I'm ready to deal with all that college crap."

He throws his arms up into the air. "It's just a tour!"

"Her future doesn't have to mean college. I never finished college, you know."

"I know, Bella, I know."

"But then, you did, didn't you? A few times."

"Bella."

"And then you moved me away from my school, my family."

And there they go, like a million times before. She had to go to work, painting murals for brats, because her parents cut her off after their little bambino mated and married a black man from the ghetto of Detroit.

"Stupido idiota," Mom utters under her breath.

"I heard that, Annabelle, but will chose to ignore it."

"Fine. Let's change the subject."

I sigh, ready to get the hell out of here. "I have to go. Chris is expecting me, like half an hour ago."

"A storm is blowing in tonight. You'd better bring an umbrella. And be careful driving," Dad cautions.

"Be vigilant, Bea. Make sure no one is following you. That Chris boy . . . he'll walk you to your car, right?"

"Yes, he will. And there will be cops everywhere."

"Well, that's good to hear." Dad sighs.

"Plus, you don't have to worry about me. I'm pretty street smart." I regret it as soon as I say it.

"What's that supposed to mean? Street smart? Richard, what does she mean by that?"

"I didn't mean anything by it! Stop reading into everything I say!"

"Okay, fine. Richard, would you pass the osso buco, please?"

"Oh, is that what this is supposed to be?" Dad says as he hands her the plate.

"Excuse me?" Mom says, standing up and knocking over her chair.

"I was just kidding . . ."

Mom storms out of the kitchen, spewing her repertoire of Italian expletives.

That is family dinner at my house.

Kumbaya, right?

• • •

I make my way down a dark tunnel toward the concession stand—the bowels of Packard High Stadium. *Shit, it's dark.* My boots stick with each step on the soda-covered, concrete floor, making me trip a little.

Something squeaks, runs by my feet. "Shit!" I yell out, my voice echoing off the walls. *There are fucking rats in here!!!*

I hurry down the tunnel, reach the stand, and pull open the heavy door. I am blinded by the stadium lights. "Chris, where are you? I can't see a thing!"

I hear his laugh and feel his hand in mine as my eyes adjust to the brightness. The high school stadium is packed. The marching band's cymbals clash, drums rattle and roll, tubas bellow. Cheerleaders flip, cartwheel, and throw one another around like rag dolls on speed. The players pump their fists, grunt, and butt their heads together.

"Holy shit. I've gone to the circus!"

"Where have you been, Beatrice Washington?" Chris scolds.

"I'm sorry, I was held against my will." I look around, down at the floor. "Do you know there are rodents running around here? Now I know why you call it Packrat High."

"You'll find that the rats are a lot nicer than the sweating ingrates I've been pouring pop for! Now come over here and let me check you out and snap a couple of quick photos before we're ambushed with orders."

"Where should I put my purse? I don't want anything furry running off with it."

"Give it to me." Chris parts the tacky gingham curtain that's hanging around the counter. "There's a little safe under here."

"Wait. I need my Moleskine." I pull it from my bag and tuck my purse away.

Chris looks me up and down through the lens of his camera. "Ooh, I love that sweater."

"So do I, but it itches like hell." *Damn. My mother was right.* "How do you like the boots?" I pose for his camera.

"Very Jane Fonda in *Barbarella*." *Click click click.* "You could make me straight, right now, the way you look."

I bat my eyes at him. "That's the sweetest thing anyone's ever said to me."

A blast of cold wind comes barreling through the concession stand like a mini-cyclone, knocking over paper cups and bags of popcorn, blowing flyers off a bulletin board.

"Brrr." Chris catches the flying debris.

"My dad said a storm was coming. At least we're under a roof in case it starts raining. You don't want to see what my hair does when it's wet."

A WANTED poster flies off the bulletin board and floats down onto the counter. A generic, bland drawing of a man's face stares up at me.

WANTED!
AGGRAVATED SEXUAL ASSAULT

"Is this the guy they think raped Willa?" I ask.

"I guess so." Chris shrugs and starts to help some customers.

I laugh. "A robot raped her?"

"What are you talking about?" he says, looking back at me.

I hold up the poster. "Chris, a kindergartner could have drawn a better face."

"They say she doesn't remember anything. I guess the police did the best they could," Chris says, making change.

"I'm sorry. He doesn't look like a real person."

"Yeah, he does kinda look like a Ken doll." Chris giggles.

"So he couldn't have raped her. Ken dolls don't have genitals."

"Mine did." Chris winks. "I drew them on."

"You whore." I play-slap him. "Well, let's see what I can do with this Ken doll."

I pull out one of the pens from my hair and shadow the nose and cheekbones, fill in his eyebrows, and sharpen his eyes. I crosshatch, adding dimension and badly needed shading.

"You like?" I show it to Chris.

"Shit, Bea, you're good. You made that face look real in a matter of seconds."

"I touched it up a little, that's all."

"But I don't know if you should be messing with a police sketch."

"Yeah, you're right." I fold and tuck the flyer into my sketchbook.

"I can't believe he's out there somewhere," Chris says, filling a bag of popcorn for a fan.

"Maybe he's here in the stadium," I whisper in his ear, "or maybe he's the man right in front of you, the one you're handing the popcorn to."

The guy walks away from the stand.

"Stop it. Stop it right now, Beatrice Washington. That's not funny, you're scaring me!"

"Oh, quit acting like a girl, *Christina*."

Chris throws a handful of popcorn at me.

The halftime buzzer blares in my ear.

"Ladies and gentleman, we now present to you our homecoming princesses!" the announcer shouts.

The fans go crazy, whooping and hollering, throwing confetti.

"Oh, please," I mutter to myself.

"Princess Sarah Alam!" the announcer burps out.

A little waif of a girl walks onto the football field, her heels sinking into the turf with each step. The gusty wind hits her hard and almost knocks her down. She stumbles, and her arms flail but find the shoulder of a kneeling football player. She safely clutches his grass-stained jersey as she's presented with a bouquet of yellow carnations.

"Princess Eva Marie Evans!" The second princess, unlike Sarah, is meaty and plows ahead like a gladiator facing a tiger in the arena. The wind wins the contest, however, as her geometric-patterned minidress balloons up over her thighs, revealing a lovely pair of Spanx. A football player presents her with a bouquet of orange carnations as he stares at her ass.

"And now, ladies and gentlemen, the moment you have all been waiting for . . . this year's Queen of Packard High!" A drumroll from the marching band: "Queen Willa Pressman!"

"Oh my gosh." Chris bounces. "She's here—look! She came! I can't believe it!" He starts snapping pictures.

"Wow. Unreal."

A spotlight shines on Willa as she steps onto the field, escorted by her weeping, proud parents. Police officers skirt the sidelines, whispering into walkie-talkies.

"Poor thing. She looks so scared," Chris says, peering through the camera lens.

Willa makes her way to midfield, the band plays something inappropriately upbeat, and the students leap to their feet with a standing ovation, applauding their queen.

A daisy-appliquéd, pink chiffon dress hangs on her bony frame and billows around her ankles in the wind. Her hair is piled high in a bun. A few wispy strands trickle down the side of her face.

Willa's parents release their hold on their daughter as the team captain presents her with a large bouquet of pink carnations—fit for a racehorse. Sarah drapes a sash around her fragile body. Eva Marie places a tiara, crookedly, on the top of her head.

Willa looks up at the stands and begins to turn in circles, around and around like a pink ballerina on a little girl's wind-up jewelry box. She waves to her adoring fans under the hot, bright wattage of the football field.

"I don't know"—I chew the tip of my pen—"I think this whole thing is sick, Chris. Raped and then crowned?"

"I think it's touching." Chris wipes a tear from his eye.

I look at Willa as she struggles with the heavy, crooked tiara, holding it in place, stopping it from falling off her head. My pen is poised, and I wait. I wonder if it'll happen again—if I'll see Marcus's face.

But no, it isn't Marcus that charges through my head. I draw a crown of thorns, digging into Willa's skull.

Chris looks over at the sketch. "What's that?"

"I don't think she likes it much, being homecoming queen."

"What are you talking about? Willa loves this. She's been campaigning for this since, like, preschool."

"I'm not too sure about that."

Eva Marie and Sarah are escorted to the side of the field, to a horse-drawn carriage adorned with hundreds of handmade pink tissue flowers. They climb on and wave to their admirers.

Willa kisses her mom and dad on the cheek and takes her boyfriend's hand, ready to step onto the carriage, when a lightning bolt cracks, brightening the purple sky.

The horses are spooked. They whinny and buck up on their hind legs, pull away from the handler, and race wildly around the track. Eva Marie and Sarah yell for help, their faces terrified.

A couple of football players chase after the carriage and finally rein in the horses at the goalpost. Sarah steps out of the carriage sobbing. Eva Marie appears to be swearing like a fullback.

A roll of booming thunder rocks the stadium stands.

Willa stands frozen on the track. Her hair, falling out of her bun now, tangles around the lopsided tiara and down her neck. Her face is stuck, twisted in horror, as if she is staring at something, someone in the crowd.

My head explodes with an image again, but not the crown of thorns and not Marcus. I pull the WANTED poster out from my Moleskine.

"Bea, what are you doing now?"

It blasts through my mind like the bolt of lightning in the sky. I see it. I draw it—a cleft, a well-defined cleft in a chin. I draw it on the face on the poster and then collapse onto a folding chair.

"Bea, what's going on? Are you okay?"

"I'm fine," I lie. "Just a little dizzy. Shit, my head hurts."

Chris hands me a cup of water. *I wish it were something stronger.*

I look at Chris and swallow. "If I tell you something, do you promise to not laugh?"

"Sure."

"And you promise you won't run away from me in fear?"

"Bea, what is it already? You're creeping me out."

"I can, like, draw things."

"Duh."

"I mean, the truth about things. I know it sounds crazy, but when I'm drawing people lately, I can see stuff when I look at them—like what they're thinking about, things that are on their minds. Like this." I hand him the WANTED poster. "The cleft in his chin. I saw it when I looked at Willa—she saw it, or she was thinking of it."

Chris laughs.

"You promised me you wouldn't laugh."

"I'm sorry, Bea. It just sounds a little Ouija board weird, a little psychic, like some sixth-sense shit. *I see dead people.*"

I shove my chilled hands into the pockets of my coat. "I'm serious, Chris. I don't know why this is happening. I can't seem to help it. And it's been happening more and more lately. Freaky, right?"

"Uh, yeah. It is. When did this start happening?"

"When I got sober—isn't that weird? I didn't understand it at rehab—I thought it was like, I don't know, a heightened sensitivity because I was clearheaded for the first time in a long time—or because I was going through withdrawal and the wiring in my brain was off. But it's still happening, and I've been sober for over three months."

Chris scrunches his forehead.

"You don't believe me, do you? Fine, I'll prove it to you." I flip through my sketchbook and turn to a page with a drawing of a guy at school who hasn't outed himself yet but should. I show it to Chris. "Who's that?" I ask.

"Ian McKinley. Why do you have a drawing of Ian in your sketchbook?"

"Because his face popped into my head when I was sketching you at lunch. Ian was on your mind—*in* your mind. Am I wrong?"

His face flushes. "Okay, that's creepy."

"Tell me about it," I say. "And it happened again in lit class, when I was taking notes during one of Mr. Kleinman's boring lectures. At first it was like static, and then it flickered. Suddenly I saw Mr. Kleinman wearing a bra, women's panties, and lipstick." I show him the sketch.

Chris doubles over in laughter. "He's a cross-dresser? Mr. Kleinman?"

"I don't want to know this about him, believe me!"

"Wow. This is pretty heavy shit. You can read people's minds?"

"It's only when I draw."

"And you're not using?"

"I'm not using! But it would probably stop if I were. This isn't a good thing, you know. I don't want to have this . . ."

"Power." Chris finishes my sentence.

Another crack of lightning, a boom of thunder. It starts to rain, hard. The soaked pink tissue flowers fall off the carriage, and the ride is nixed. Willa's dad covers her with his coat as they rush to the sidelines. Umbrellas pop open, and the concession stand is mobbed under the awning. I jump up, put my sketchbook down on the counter, and join Chris, pouring sodas, filling bags of popcorn, and making change, earning our service-learning hours as orders are tossed out:

"Milk Duds! Do you have Milk Duds?"

"My popcorn is wet . . . I need another!"

"I wanted diet pop, and this tastes like it has sugar in it!"

"You gave me the wrong change, you moron."

The buzzer blares, and the players continue on with the game, rain and all. The concession stand clears. I plop down on the chair, rub my feet, itch my arms, and begin to regret that I told my only friend in the world the weird truth about me.

"Talk about crazy!" Chris sighs.

"The crowd or me?"

"Both." He laughs.

"I probably shouldn't have told you. Promise me you'll still be my friend?"

"Move over." I do, and he sits on the corner of the chair. "Bea, I will always be your friend, no matter what."

I turn to him, almost falling off, so he puts me on his lap and scratches my itchy back. "I don't expect you to understand. I don't. I mean, I don't even understand myself. It's, like, not normal."

"Normal? What's *normal*? We all have stuff."

I kiss him on the cheek. "Thanks."

"For what?"

"For not running away."

"A Diet Coke for Willa! Fast! Hurry!" Eva Marie barks. Willa and her ladies of the court stand at the concession stand.

"Of course," Chris says.

Sarah asks for a cup of water.

"That was horrible, what happened with the horses." I hand Willa the pop.

"Are you okay?" Chris asks the girls.

Willa, still wearing her father's coat, looks down at the counter, at my open sketchbook, at the modified WANTED poster, and gasps. "Who did that? Who drew on that?"

"Who did what?" Chris asks.

"Drew on that—that face?" Willa points at the flyer.

"I did," I confess.

Chris mouths, "Uh-oh."

Willa chokes up. "Are you mocking me? Are you making fun of what happened to me?"

"Oh god, no. I'm so sorry. I was just playing with it a little," I sputter.

"Give it to me!" She grabs it.

"That's an official police sketch, not a coloring book!" Eva Marie barks. "Are you nuts?"

Willa looks at me. Her voice drops down a half-octave. "Who are you, anyway?"

"She's the new druggie girl at school. A rehab rat," Eva Marie snorts.

"My name is Bea, Bea Washington," I correct her. "And yes, I'm new at the school. And I'm sorry, I'm really sorry I drew on the poster." I glance at Chris, hoping for some support.

He mimes closing a zipper on my mouth.

The school photographer approaches the girls and saves my sorry ass. "We're ready to take pictures now, in the gym."

"Oh! I must look like a wet rat," Willa panics. "I need a mirror."

"We'll go with you," Eva Marie chimes in. Sarah nods in agreement.

Willa squints her baby blues at me one last time as she pops open an umbrella and walks up the stairs of the stadium toward the gymnasium.

Eva Marie hands me an empty cup. "Bitch." She marches off and joins her queen.

"Open mouth, insert stiletto," Chris quips.

"Hey, Chris, cover for me?" I grab my bag from the safe. "I need a smoke, like, big time."

"You know, you really should quit."

"I know, I know, it's a nasty habit."

"I'm not going to want to kiss you on our first date with your mouth tasting like an ashtray."

"I'm crushed."

"You should be. I'll have to save it for Ian, I guess."

"Hey, thanks again for not bolting on me . . . with what I told you before."

"Are you kidding me? I'm going to use you. Win the lottery with your power."

"Shut up."

• • •

I walk fast up the dark ramp, using my phone as a flashlight, hopefully scaring off the critters. I step out of the tunnel and into the parking lot. The wind scoops in and inverts my umbrella. *Shit.* I know my hair is skyrocketing to the moon, so I duck back into the tunnel, lean against the wall, and take a cigarette out of my bag.

"Need a light?"

I startle at a figure, a man standing next to me in the shadows. A cigarette lighter flicks on in the darkness.

"Who the fuck are you?"

He lowers his cap, and a shiny badge reading POLICE glistens in the dark.

"Oh! I'm sorry I swore, officer." *Just what I need, trouble with a cop.* I hide my cigarette.

"Well, do you or don't you want a light?"

"You sure?" I ask.

He nods.

"Um, thanks." I put the cigarette in my mouth, and he lights it, then lights his own, illuminating his eyes for a fraction of a second.

He exhales. "You know, you shouldn't be out here all alone."

"I know. I have a buddy down in the concession stand. Just needed a smoke."

We stand in silence.

Okay . . . this is awkward.

"Shouldn't you be patrolling, looking for bad guys or something?"

"I'd rather be here with you."

"Um . . . I'm going to go to the little girl's room."

"I'll walk you there."

"No, thank you. I think I'll be fine."

"Okay, be careful. I wouldn't want anything to happen to you."

"Yeah, well, thanks again for the light."

I jog through the rain to the back entrance of the school and turn when I get to the door, stubbing out my cigarette with my boot. He's still standing there in the tunnel, the red embers of his lit cigarette like a firefly in the darkness.

Talk about a creepy cop!

I push open the door. The hallway is empty. My heels click and echo on the tiled floor as I walk into the ladies' room.

It's dark. I flip a switch. The fluorescent lights flicker on with a buzz. I look in the mirror, at my crazed hair, and sigh at the mess. The door suddenly slams open. I turn, ready to kick the creep in the balls with my "don't fuck with me" boots.

"How do you know him?" She stands there, wet and shivering.

"Willa, you scared the shit out of me."

Willa locks the door. She holds the WANTED poster in her hands. "I said, how do you know him?"

She's a little wobbly and looks scared. The bruises on her neck stand out under the fluorescent lights, and all of a sudden I feel like hugging her.

"I don't know him. I was playing around on the poster.

It was stupid of me. I'm into art, it's what I do—draw."

She walks toward me—her eyes wild, pupils dilated. "So you don't know him. You've never seen him?"

"Does that look like him? The guy who raped you? Did you see him here tonight, in the stands?"

"How the hell would I know?" I smell her breath. The sweet, familiar odor wafts my way and fills my pierced nostrils. She turns, looks into the mirror, and straightens her crown. "I don't remember anything from that night." Willa takes makeup out of her bag and touches up the bruises on her neck.

"Does it still hurt? Your neck?"

"What do you think?"

A little blood trickles out of her nose and lands on an embroidered daisy on her dress.

"Um, your nose. It's . . . I think it's bleeding."

Willa dabs the blood with the corner of a wet paper towel and glares at me through the mirror.

We couldn't be less similar, Willa and me. My dark, ethnic look; her fair, all-American look. And yet, at that moment, standing side by side, looking at each other through the mirror, we are one and the same.

And then I see it—like a little light clicking on in her head. She knows I know, and I know that she knows I know.

"I can try and help you, Willa. I can, if you want."

"What are you talking about? *You* help *me*?"

I hear Eva Marie and Sarah in the hallway. "Willa? Willa? Are you okay? You in there?" they yell, pounding on the door.

I jot my cell phone number on the flyer and hand it back to her. "I'm here if you need me."

Willa looks down at my number, folds the flyer, and slips it into her purse. She unlocks the door, and the girls fall into the room. They stop when they see me and make a face like they smell something bad.

"Are you okay?" Sarah hugs Willa. "We couldn't find you. We were so worried."

"I'm fine—let's get our pictures taken."

The door slams in my face.

• • •

My windshield wipers work hard while I drive home, and the wind whistles, bending saplings alongside the road in half. I sit a little forward in my seat, slow down, and concentrate on the wet, slick road ahead of me.

Jesus, what a night, I think to myself. *Willa was tweaked, no question. And the face on the poster, with the shading I did, the cleft I drew . . . it must look like him. Why doesn't she want anyone to know that she remembers him?*

A light floods my rearview mirror, shining bright in my eyes. *What the . . . ?* I adjust the mirror and see a car behind me. The lights barrel toward me, pulling up close.

"Shit," I say out loud. "What's their hurry?"

I speed up, thinking I'm driving too slowly. But the car speeds up with me and is now tailgating me—dangerously close.

My street is coming up ahead, on the right. I wait until the last second, without turning my blinker on, and pull the steering wheel hard to the right. My tires screech and fishtail as they follow my order. The car behind me turns and screeches along with me, speeding up, getting even closer. The bright lights shine and flicker in my eyes.

"OH MY GOD! It's going to hit me!"

I abruptly turn left, careening into my driveway. I slam on my brakes with both feet, and the menacing car speeds off into the darkness.

Holy shit. I try to collect my breath.

My cell rings in my purse. My heart won't stop racing.

I take a deep breath and answer. "Hello." The phone wobbles in my shaky hands.

A slurred voice. "Monday, before school at seven. The antique barn on Lilac Lane. Meet me—"

"Willa? Is that you? Was that you following me?"

She hangs up.

• • •

The storm continues outside my window as I stand in my bathroom, looking in the mirror. *Beatrice Beaver-head, Chia Pet Washington.* I pull my hair back into a ponytail and see the scared hazel eyes of a little Bea hiding behind heavy, dark eyeliner. I spread a glob of Vaseline on those eyes, coating and covering all the dirt, the filth, the seedy alleys of my life. I wipe off the grime with a cotton ball, soiling the pure white fluff with the blackness of my soul. I stare at my naked, greasy face in the mirror.

It started when I was in the eighth grade. I was thirteen and away on a school trip to Cedar Point Amusement Park, about an hour away in Ohio.

I was in my Beaver-head phase. Trying my hardest to look like one of the pretty girls at Athena Day. I would flatiron my shoulder-length hair every morning, burning the crap out of it, making it frizz even more.

We had assigned seats on the bus—a failed attempt by the teachers to break up some of the mean-girl cliques at the school. I was next to Agatha. Agatha Rand. Not only one of the prettiest girls in the school but one of the most popular, and for sure, one of the richest.

Agatha wasn't too happy about sitting by me, and she made that abundantly clear. She talked on her cell phone for most of the ride with her best friend, Marissa, who was sitting ten rows ahead of us, until one of the teachers, Miss Metzler, confiscated her phone.

"That bitch," she muttered.

"I know, right?" I commiserated.

Agatha looked at me, surprised, as if she just noticed I was there. She dug through her purse and took out a tiny little white envelope and hid it on her lap, in the pleats of her uniform skirt. She pulled out a foiled sheet of pills.

"What are you looking at?" she asked.

"Nothing." I looked away and started drawing in my sketchbook.

Agatha leaned over and watched me sketch Miss Metzler with a fat ass and clown lips. She cracked up. "That's hilarious!"

"Thanks," I said, trying to hide my smile.

"Hey," Agatha whispered. "You ever done speed?"

"Uh, no."

"Want to now?"

I shrugged. "I don't know. What will it feel like?"

"Not very different. It'll make things go a little faster, make the rides a little more fun. We could do a roller coaster together." She laughed to herself. "Riding on ice would be bitchin'!"

"Really? You and me? On the roller coaster?"

"Sure, why not?"

"Okay, why not?" I giggled and closed my sketchbook.

And that was it. That's all it took.

I was hooked from that moment on, to Agatha and to any drug I could get my hands on. And she had plenty of them.

I became more relaxed with myself as the eighth grade continued on. It's when I let my hair go wild and free, pierced my nose, rolled my uniform skirt up to my butt cheeks, discovered my retro look, and became one of the cool girls—and Aggie's best friend.

• • •

I jump at the loud knock on my bedroom door.

"Bea!!! Bea, let us in!!!" my parents yell.

I open the door and they stand there, looking as if the air's been sucked out of them, like two deflated balloons.

"Aggie. Agatha Rand," Mom squeaks, tears streaming down her face.

"What? What about Aggie? What's wrong? Dad?"

"She's the girl who was missing," he says.

"Oh, no! Is she okay? Is Aggie okay?" I yell.

My dad reaches out, holding on to my shoulders. "No, Bea. She's dead. Agatha is dead. They think it was an overdose."

I pass out, collapsing into his arms.

Darkness.

3 months 7 days 12 hours

The storm has blown over Ann Arbor, spitting its way east toward Lake Huron and into Canada. High, blustery clouds float weightlessly in the scrubbed-clean, blue gray sky.

It's Sunday. I'm still numb and speechless with the news of Aggie's death, but Jewish tradition dictates burying the body as soon after death as possible, as a mark of respect. I sit in the backseat of my parent's car as we drive to the funeral.

"I heard more from campus police. They don't think any foul play was involved," Dad says. "Agatha was found fully clothed, lying in the grass on Wave Field."

"On campus, Dad? They found her on campus?"

"They did."

My stomach jolts.

I can't share with my parents that I saw her at the frat house with Marcus on the night she died. They thought I was at a meeting, and they'd probably throw me back into rehab, even though I didn't take the pills from Marcus.

It eats away at me. *I could have helped her. I should have helped her, but I was so pissed at her and Marcus.* The tears start welling up in my eyes again, and I wipe them with my black-knit blanket poncho and stare at the clouds outside the car window.

I wish I were on top of one of the clouds. Floating away, away . . .

I hear the somber chords of a pipe organ as we walk up to the mortuary. We find a seat in the back. My mom and dad bookend me, shielding me from potential looks and stares. Fellow ex-classmates, the girls from Athena Day, huddle in the front pews, crying, hugging one another.

Aggie's parents sit by her coffin. Her mom sobs, her mouth reciting prayers as if she's in a séance, summoning Aggie to rise up from the dead.

My mom draws me in close and softly cries.

I spot Maria, Aggie's housekeeper. Her face is buried in a lace hankie. I miss Maria, miss her sweet, understanding eyes.

A slide show begins on a high screen in the front of the room. Dozens of blown-up pictures of a happy, carefree Aggie throughout the years flash above: Aggie as a pudgy, adorable baby; her toddler years; her birthday parties. Aggie in middle school. I recognize the picture of our tenth-grade school camping trip—river rafting down the Indian River in northern Michigan. Aggie and I had so much fun, but we were blasted. I see my hand—the silver ring I wear on my thumb—it rests on Aggie's shoulder. But my body, my face, is cut out.

Our eleventh-grade class picture—all forty of us—is displayed on the screen. Aggie stands in the middle, her big, toothy smile framed by her curly hair. I stand next to her—but my face, my face is blotted out with black ink. It's obvious to me that I am cut out, obliterated out of every single picture.

I don't understand. Why? Why am I not in any of the pictures? I didn't do anything wrong!

My chest swells with emotion—deep, deep sadness and hurt—and a long-overdue sob gushes out of me, echoing off the marble walls of the mortuary.

The girls whisper, nudge each other—some of them turn around. I feel eyes burning into me—judging, hateful, piercing.

I make eye contact with Aggie's mom. She turns and whispers something to her husband. Probably saying, "What is she doing here? That druggie!"

My head feels like it's going to explode off my body, like in the pictures, and I untangle myself from my mom's arms and stand, crying out, "I didn't do anything wrong. I didn't! She was my friend, my best friend. I belong in those pictures, too!"

The organist stops, holding a sustained minor chord. Mr. Rand stands, looks at me—anger fills his red-rimmed eyes.

I bolt out of the mortuary.

My parents follow, calling out to me, "Bea, Bea, please stop!"

I run across the street, pass Aggie's hearse—and a car nearly hits me. I continue, fast, into a woody ravine. I don't feel my legs as they move through the muddy thicket. I don't feel the dense, leafless trees scratching at me, pulling at my hair. I keep running faster and faster to I don't know where.

The creek stops me—the creek where Willa was found—and I fall to the ground, crying, wailing, wanting to die, wanting to end it all. Rolling around in wet, rotting leaves.

Why wasn't it me? Why not me?

"That wasn't fair of them," he pants, out of breath. "You being cut out of the pictures."

I peek through my fingers covered in mud and leaves.

Marcus.

He crouches down.

"What . . . are . . . you . . . doing . . . here?" My breath spasms.

He holds his chest, places his arms underneath his pits, breathing hard. "I figured they wouldn't have been happy to see me either, but I had to come. It's so sad—so sad about Aggie. I hid in the back and followed you. Thought you'd never stop. I didn't know you could run so fast!"

I hop up to my knees, grab him by his shoulders, and yell, "You killed her! You killed Aggie!!!"

He takes hold of my hands, stops me. "No, Bea, I didn't.

She didn't OD with me. Aggie left like an hour after you. I made her tea, she ate some crackers, and she left."

"I don't believe you," I hiss at him, standing, pulling away from his grasp. I back up into the trunk of a birch tree.

Marcus stands. "Hey, hey . . . what's going on? Huh?" He walks toward me. "We had something good going on the other night . . ."

He leans in and tries to hug me. I reach up and snap a branch off the tree and swing it around, whipping his legs.

He flinches. "What the . . . ? What the hell is wrong with you?"

I circle him, threatening him with the stick. "You gave her the drugs, didn't you, after you fucked her!"

"Hey, calm down. We didn't have sex. She's just a friend, I told you that."

"But you gave her the drugs!"

"Yeah, I gave her some shit. But not enough to kill her. It's not my damn fault!"

"It's never your fault is it, Marcus? Wasn't your fault with me . . ."

"Give me a break. You were using before I met you."

He tries to get a hold of the branch. And I flip it around, whipping it in the air. "Wasn't your fault with Willa . . ."

"Shit, I had nothing to do with that."

I continue circling him like a crazed animal. "Can you prove it? Can you? You fucking her, too?"

"That cunt? Never."

I cringe and take a swing at him. The branch slaps his face and draws blood.

He touches his wound, looks at the blood on his fingers. "Shit. You're acting crazy, Bea. Give me that."

He wrestles it from my hands and throws it far into the woods. "Now, come on . . . you're upset, I get it . . ."

"I'm more than upset, Marcus," I hiss. "That girl, that girl in the Arb last spring . . ."

I close my eyes. The smell of the wet grass, the heaviness of my weighted-down body, her voice—*help me, help me!* comes rushing back. "When I heard her . . . when I woke up, I couldn't find you—you weren't there, Marcus. You weren't there."

He laughs. "You were messed up. I was with you the whole time."

"Art class—first day of school at Packard High, looking at Willa . . . I saw your face. She was thinking of you—you were on her mind."

"Bea, what are you going on about?" Marcus walks toward me.

"Don't touch me! I'll call the cops if you try." I dive for my purse, my phone.

Marcus tries to snatch it from me. I kick his hand away. He shakes it in pain. "Damn! That hurts!"

"Did you rape them? Did you kill them?"

"No! Of course not! You're wrong, Bea, dead wrong!"

"Well, why don't we let the police decide that!"

He throws his arms up in the air and starts backing away. "Fine. I won't touch you. I'll leave you alone, if that's what you want. Just put the damn phone away."

"Bea!!!" We both look up at the sound of my mom's voice. "Where are you, Bea? Bea!!!"

"I didn't do it. Any of it. I didn't." Marcus turns from me, hops over the creek, and walks off, deep into the woods.

3 months
8 days
7 hours

It's early Monday morning. I am exhausted, bone tired. But I drive down Lilac Lane. It's a dirt road, and the mud puddles splash and muck up my windshield.

An old red antique barn is at the end of the lane. I step out of my car and into a puddle wearing my suede ankle boots.

Damn.

I hopscotch past the puddles and push at a heavy wood door that doesn't want to budge. An old cowbell hangs to the right of the door. I pull its chain. The clanging disrupts a gaggle of pigeons on the overhead eaves, and they flutter and poop.

Crap.

I find a couple of tissues in the pocket of my new velvet coat and wipe some of the bird shit off my shoulders. God only knows what the top of my head looks like.

There's no way I'm ringing that cowbell again. So I push

the door, hard, using all my weight, and it opens. I'm hit with the strong smell of dust and mold, and sneeze.

"Willa? Willa, are you here?" I call out.

The shop is dim, lit by the open front door. I step in a little farther and trip. The heel of my right boot breaks off on an old iron doorstop—a squirrel with an acorn in its mouth.

Shit.

I drop the heel of my boot into my oversized flap bag and hobble through the shop with my arms outstretched like a lame blind woman.

"Willa, answer me!" I call out.

I walk right into a spiderweb, brush it off, lose my balance, and fall onto an antique velvet sofa. A naked sewing mannequin plops down on my lap.

Fuck.

Her blank, glassy button eyes stare up at me as if she were the one surprised with our encounter. I push the naked dummy off my lap and stumble to the back of the shop, open a rusted screen door that's screaming of tetanus and step into the backyard.

Willa sits on a huge tree stump. She looks like an ad in a Macy's catalog, wearing a baby blue velour Juicy Couture tracksuit, a down-feather vest, and smoking a joint.

I hobble over to a dirty iron bench and sit.

Willa takes a hit. She holds it in for a second, then releases a steady, graceful, gray stream of smoke—like cool, liquid silver.

She holds out the joint. "Want some?"

"You have no idea how much I do," I answer. "But no, no thank you."

"Whatever." Willa fingers the top of the stump. "They cut off chickens' heads on this thing."

"Well, that's creepy. Why are you sitting on it?"

Willa shrugs. "Feels appropriate." She takes another hit off the joint, squinting her eyes. "What did you say to Marcus?"

"What are you talking about?"

Willa snaps at me. "He texted me, told me to never contact him again. I asked him why and he said it had something to do with you—something you said to him. And now he won't answer my calls! What did you say to him?"

"So you admit you know him."

"Why the hell do you care if I do? Just get him back—I *need* him back."

"Is he the one who raped you, Willa?"

"What?" She starts laughing. "Is that what you said to him? Christ. No wonder. No, you idiot, of course he didn't rape me!"

"He didn't, you're positive?"

"It wasn't Marcus, okay? He's at least three inches shorter than the—"

Willa catches herself and steps off the stump.

"I thought you didn't remember anything—who he was, what he looked like."

"This was a mistake, calling you here. You don't understand."

"What don't I understand?"

She turns on me. "I'm homecoming queen! I'm dating the captain of the football team! I'm an honor student! I'm going Ivy League! If they find him—"

"You'll get found out?" I cut her off like a chicken head on the stump. "Is that what you're so afraid of, being found out?"

She licks her fingers, snuffs out the joint, takes a pack of cigarettes out of her jacket pocket, exchanges the joint for a smoke, and plops down on the wet ground. The mud must be soaking through her pants, but it doesn't seem to bother her. She lights up.

I reach out. "*That* I will take a hit of. I ran out."

Willa hands me her cigarette. She wipes her pert nose with her sleeve, settles back, and leans against the bloody stump, staring at me. "So you don't use anymore?" she asks.

I take a deep inhale. "No, haven't for three months."

She pauses. "Nothing? Not even weed?"

"Nothing." I exhale.

"Is it hard?"

"Hard?" I laugh. "You ever try to stop a semi truck coming at you full speed? Like every day? Every hour? Every minute? Yeah, it's hard, but better than where I was, I guess."

"What, are you some kind of superhero?"

"Right. My cape is in my bag." I hand her back the cigarette.

"It's like you saw through me or something the other night."

"Do you want to be seen, Willa?"

"What are you talking about?"

"I see that you've been hiding behind lies for years now. You hate the crown they've placed on your head, all the expectations, all those labels you just threw at me."

"You're wrong."

"Am I? Well, why don't you try taking the crown off for a minute? See how it feels. Let's see who Willa really is."

"Why would I do that?"

"Why *wouldn't* you? It doesn't impress me—you being a homecoming queen, all that Ivy League–bound shit."

"Fuck you." Willa nibbles on her nail.

"He raped you! He beat you—thought you were dead—*wanted* you dead. And he killed that girl, last spring in the Arb. He's out there—he has to be stopped—and *you* are the only one who can stop him!"

Willa stands up, stubs out her smoke in the mud, and kicks the stump. "Okay, okay, okay, shut up!" she stammers. "You want to know the truth? Do you? You're right! I hate myself!" She starts slapping her face. "I do! I hate Willa the queen! I hate Willa the cheerleader! I hate Willa the honor student! Willa the perfect daughter! I hate her! I despise her!"

"It must be hard, all those expectations."

"And you know what?" She wipes the tears off her face, smearing mascara around like war paint. "I deserved it, what happened to me."

"No. No, no . . . you did not deserve to be raped! Never, ever think that!"

She paces back and forth. "I flirted with him! I got into his car! I asked him to buy the vodka—and I was doped up on benzos—fucked up, not him."

"Are you afraid he'll blow your cover? Is that it? Is that what you're worried about?"

The corners of her mouth turn down and quiver. "He was good-looking—nice clothes, cool car. He was supposed to take me for a short ride, like a half hour. A little flirting around is all I thought! I was so stupid!"

"It wasn't your fault, Willa, none of it."

"Yes, it was! Don't you see?"

"You can't blame yourself. You can't. And *no one* will blame you. I promise you that."

Willa climbs her way back on top of the bloody stump, closes her eyes.

I open my Moleskine, and I hear Willa's story—the truth. The truth about what happened to her that horrible night.

• • •

It was a humid September afternoon. Willa started home from cheerleading practice with good intentions—but instead found herself pulling into a corner liquor store parking lot.

She had already popped a few downers, and was feeling pretty mellow. Her car idled as she clicked her nails on the steering wheel, eyed the customers going in and out of the store, looked for the right person; she'd know when she spotted him.

A black convertible BMW pulled up. A handsome guy at the wheel looked over at her and pushed his dark hair out of his eyes. Willa knew she found what she was looking for and smiled, lowering her head and looking up at him with her heavy-lidded baby blues.

He rolled down the passenger-side window. "Hi."

"Hi," Willa answered. "Nice car."

"Thanks."

"How old are you?" she asked.

"How old do you want me to be?"

"Old enough to buy me vodka?" Willa held a twenty out her window.

"Sure, but only if it's my treat."

She put the twenty back into her purse. "Well, aren't you the gentleman. Thank you."

"You're welcome. What's your name?"

"Willa. What's yours?"

"Designated driver?" He leaned over and opened the passenger door of his car, gesturing for Willa to join him.

"You'll give me a ride in this?"

"The ride of your life." He chuckled.

"Wow. That's so cool."

Willa stepped out of her car, grabbed her pom-pom, and tickled him on the chin as she joined him. He smiled, pushed his hair away from his eyes again, and cued the music on his car stereo to Nirvana. Keeping the car idling, he walked into the store to buy the vodka.

Holy shit, what a catch, Willa said to herself as she pulled down the mirror on the visor above her. It lit up, illuminating her face. She freshened her lip gloss, pressed the seat warmer button, and melted with delight. The door opened, and she pushed up the visor.

"Cheers." He handed her a bottle in a paper bag.

Willa screwed open the top of the bottle in the paper bag, not even looking at the label, took a swig, coughed a little, and handed it to him.

"I told you, I'm your designated driver."

"Your loss." She sipped.

He pressed a button, and the convertible top started rolling down.

She giggled. "It's supposed to rain, you know."

"You afraid of a little rain?" he asked.

"I'm not afraid of anything," Willa said as she released her hair from her ponytail.

The car started off down the road, and her long blond hair blew up into the wind. She looked at the sky—blurry stars sparkled from behind the dark clouds. She relaxed, crossed her legs.

"You have beautiful legs. Long, strong, lean," he said.

Willa smiled at him, and her cell phone rang. "Shit, it's my mom." She answered in a sweet voice, "Hi, Mom. Sorry

I didn't call you. Practice ran a little late. I'll be home in about"—Willa looked at him—"a half hour?" He nodded. "Yeah, a half hour, Mom, no later. Okay, love you, too."

Willa put her phone in her purse. Eager to resume the vodka buzz, she took another gulp, sighed, and closed her eyes.

"What did you say your name was again?" she purred.

• • •

Willa continues on with the story, her arms hugging her knees into her chest as she rocks on the tree stump. "And he turned left, onto that road, into the gulley. I was like, 'wait, where are you going?' It started to rain. I asked him to close the top of the car, and he was like a . . . robot. Like so stiff and unresponsive. He clenched his jaw, and his lips looked like a couple of ugly worms. He parked the car by the creek and turned to me. His eyes were dark, as dark as the sky that night. And he had, like, a thing on his chin."

"A cleft?"

"Yeah, a cleft. I jumped out of the car, tried to run, but I slipped. He tackled me and started beating me, and then he dragged me down by the creek. And I was so high, numb—I was so messed up, I couldn't fight him, I couldn't. He put something on my eyes—a scarf—blindfolded me, tied my arms and wrapped something around me, so tight I couldn't breathe. And I kept hearing—a noise . . . a weird noise."

"What did you hear?"

"I don't know, like something whirring and clicks."

"Whirring?"

"Over and over—fast, whirring and clicking. But I don't know—he boxed my ears pretty hard, so I had no idea what it was. And then it stopped, and that's when he . . ."

"That's when he raped you?"

Willa nods. "He choked me, and I couldn't breathe—I just wanted it to be over. I forced my body to go limp, to let go. I prayed to die. Oh my god—I knew I was going to die!"

"But you didn't, Willa, you didn't die."

Willa sobs, her body trembles, shivers. "But don't you see? It was my fault, it was all my fault. I was so messed up . . . I never should have . . ."

This is the second time I have the urge to hug her. Instead, I drape my paisley velvet coat around her shoulders. And I take her face into my hands and force her to look at me. "Everything is going to be okay. You're doing the right thing, Willa, you are. You're going to be okay."

She breaks our stare, severing the connection between us, and looks down, into the face I drew in the sketchbook.

His face stares up at us. A face I do not remember drawing—a face that possessed me, possessed my hand—took over my pen. Drawn with her words, her thoughts, what she saw—the truth.

"No, no, no, no," she says over and over again as her whole body starts to quiver. And she looks at me as if I'm the enemy.

I see that little light going on again, the way every addict ignites a lie, an alibi. Willa hops off the stump; her tears stop and morph into even, controlled breaths as she states, "That's not him. I made it up, you fool—all of it. I wanted to see how far you would go with this. You're a hack, a loser." She flips her hair.

"What? Willa, wait . . . you're scared, I understand. What you said—what I drew—was the truth."

"According to who? You? An addict? A rehab rat? Gee, people will really believe you over me." She laughs at the realization. "As I told the police, I don't remember anything. Nothing. Nothing about him. Now, give me that sketch." Willa holds out her hand.

"No," I say. "No, I don't believe you. You want help—you need help."

Willa yanks my sketchbook from my hands and rips out the page. She looks at it coolly and tears it in half, in quarters, into tiny pieces as it falls to the ground. "We never met here, you got that? And if you tell anyone about today, about what happened here, I promise I will nail your skinny, black ass."

"I can help you. Please, please let me help."

"Get your own help, you weirdo."

Willa walks away with my coat still draped around her shoulders, past the antique barn, and into her car, speeding off—leaving me, and the shredded pieces of the rapist—in the mud.

• • •

A blinking yellow light flashes ahead of me at the intersection, cautioning me as I mull over which way I should go.

Right toward the police station.

Left toward school.

What the hell am I thinking? Walking into a police station? Me? Willa will deny everything. And what do I have to show them, anyway? A ripped-up sketch of a man who Willa said didn't rape her!

Nope. There's no way I should walk into that station. No way.

The traffic light continues to blink.

Turn right.

Turn left.

I look at the sketch of the crown of thorns, which is sitting open on the seat next to me.

Shit. She's miserable and in pain. She's calling out to me for help. I didn't help the girl in the Arb; I didn't help Aggie. I have *to help Willa.* A car honks behind me.

I turn right, toward the police station.

• • •

I keep setting the metal detector off. I take the earrings out of my lobes, the bangles off my wrist, my rhinestone belt, my silver ring . . . and the damn metal detector *still* goes off.

"You think it could be my nose ring?" I *so* do not want to be strip-searched by this female officer.

"Take it off and we'll see," she orders.

"Oh, man, if I take it out, it'd be a bitch to get it back in. Don't you have a wand thingy—like what they use at the airport?"

She sighs. "Fine, step to the side."

I do, and she passes the wand thingy over my body, traveling up and down my torso, between my legs, under my armpits—very awkward.

"Um . . . the nose ring is in my nose," I remind her.

She fondles the police badge pinned on her shirt and glares at me.

I see my fuzzy reflection in the thick Plexiglas divider behind her and I shut up. I look like a street person. I'm soaked, no coat, wet shoes—one without a heel. I have filthy hands, and bird poop is glued to my frizzy hair. I feel the need to explain myself. "I'm normally well put together. An hour ago my hair was lying vertically, not horizontally, and my boots? They used to be suede; now they look like cardboard. And I was wearing a fabulous coat, but she took it for some reason."

Officer lady *so* doesn't give a shit and suppresses a yawn—her nostrils flare.

"The reason I'm here is because I have to talk to someone about the Willa Pressman case. The girl who was raped? It's very important."

The wand thingy goes nuts as she passes it by my nose. I bite my tongue, wanting to say, "Told ya so."

She sighs. "You're free to go."

I look around the station. "But, um, where *do* I go?"

"See that jolly-looking fellow behind the desk?" She points. "Go share your very important information with him. I'm sure he'll love to hear your story."

I look over and see a three-hundred-pound, toady-looking man. "Him?" I ask.

She nods and belly laughs.

"Okay, I'll do that, I guess. If I have to." I swallow. "Thank you, though. Thanks for not kicking me out . . . with the way I look."

She's obviously not used to many thank-yous during her day and looks down at her pudgy feet in her sensible shoes and shifts her weight.

I gather up my metal paraphernalia, dump it into my bag, and hobble over to Mr. Toad. I close my eyes, take a deep breath, and say, "I would like to talk to somebody about the Willa Pressman case. I think I may have some new information for them."

"Down the hallway, on the left. The name Sergeant Daniels is on the door." He grunts. "But I wouldn't rush in; knock first." He leans in close, like he's about to tell me a secret, and hands me a lollipop. "Don't let her know I'm not mean." He looks at the female cop and laughs. "It's a game with me . . . keeps her squirming. I like seeing her squirm," he rasps.

"Okay, thanks." I unwrap the lollipop—orange, my

favorite, and now that I think of it, my breakfast—and pop it into my mouth.

"Remember to knock first," he croaks.

The uneven sound of my heels echoes off the cold cinderblock walls as I clunk down the hallway. Not wanting to disturb any serious police business, I take my boots off, mourn their condition one last time, and stuff them into my bag. I continue down the hall, cautiously shoeless.

I come to a closed door, and like Mr. Toad promised, "Sergeant Daniels" is spelled out in tarnished brass letters.

Daniels. The name rings a bell. Detective Daniels. *Oh, shit.*

Athena Day School for Girls—fall, eleventh grade—a year ago. It was an assembly day—"Just Say No to Drugs Day." A Detective Daniels was the guest speaker, and I'm sure he felt pretty lucky walking into a high school packed with hundreds of horny teenaged girls in uniforms—he being the only male on the premises. And I vaguely remember that he was sort of cute, in a tall, blond kind of way. Giggles erupted when he walked in accompanied by Sally, a drug-sniffing beagle.

"Shit," Aggie said to me. "He brought a canine with him."

"You're not carrying, are you?" I asked.

"Just a bag. But damn, I heard those mutts sniff out as little as a seed. Here, Bea, you take care of it." She stuffed the baggie into my backpack.

"Aggie! That's not fair! What am I supposed to do with it?"

Miss Roberts, our bio teacher, walked by. "Um, may I please use the bathroom?"

"After the assembly, Beatrice. You'll have to wait. We're about to begin."

"But I started"—I feigned embarrassment—"you know, Aunt Flow's come to visit."

"Who's visiting you, dear?"

You'd think a biology teacher would've understood the reference. "Um, I have to go ride the cotton pony?"

"I do not know what you are talking about, Miss Washington. Now take a seat."

"My period!" I blurted out. "I've started my period!"

Of course all the girls heard this, and having a man in the room made the giggles even louder. And Miss Roberts, embarrassed in front of Detective Daniels, dismissed me as the beagle started sniffing the air, following a scent, walked directly toward me, and bayed.

Aggie gave me the thumbs-up, and I was out of that auditorium lickety-split, before the dog blew my cover and revealed Aggie's stash. I threw myself into the nearest bathroom, stuffed the plastic bag under a pile of paper towels in the wastebasket, dumped a wad of fresh towels on top, and prayed that the janitor wouldn't clean up before I could get it back to Aggie.

My prayers went unanswered, as later in the day, after finally making it back to the bathroom, I found the trash can empty, a new, clean plastic liner clinging to its sides. Aggie was so pissed at me for ditching her weed. "What were you thinking? A trash can? Come on!" She didn't talk to me for a week, and to make matters worse, I did start my period.

I cursed the detective and his dog that day and now wonder if it's the same cop I'm about to meet, and if he's been promoted to sergeant, and if I'll be sniffed out again.

"Get down on the ground, hands above your head. Now!" a man's voice demands through the cheap plywood door.

I knock.

A series of gunshots flies through the air. I instinctively duck; my knees hit the door, and it inches open.

Peeking through the crack, expecting to see something gnarly going on, I instead spot two grown men playing an interactive video game—Manhunt. They are pointing their remote controls like guns, shooting and swearing at the screen in front of them.

"Got him!" a tall, lanky cop celebrates. (Yeah, it's the same Daniels.) "I blew you away, Cole!"

"No way, Daniels, you missed him—you hit the dummy!" The shorter cop taunts, "I set you up, you fool!" He performs a little jig around the room.

"Did not!"

"Did too!"

"OH MY GOD," I say. And all the fear, the anxiety of confronting the "men in blue" evaporates. The shorter cop, the trigger-happy one, turns and points the remote at me, ready to obliterate my existence.

I raise my hands in the air and feign fright. "Please, please, please don't shoot me. I'm a good guy—really, I am."

The tall cop laughs a little. "Detective Cole, put your weapon, uh, I mean, the remote down." He turns the video game off, smoothes his blond hair, rubs his almond-shaped green eyes, and attempts to look important, sound important. "Uh, I'm Sergeant Daniels, he's Detective Cole. Can we help you?"

"I hope so, but after that, I have my doubts." I hold out my hand—my cold, dirty hand. "Bea. Beatrice Washington." Sergeant Daniels takes it without hesitation.

"And you're here because . . . ?" the sergeant asks.

I don't have time to fool around. I have no idea how I'll explain my lengthy absence from school, so I march over to his desk and dump out the contents of my bag. The wet shoes come clumping out first, then my wallet. The jewelry, pens, my sketchbook are tossed out with the torn pieces of the sketch.

"What do you think you're doing?" Detective Cole approaches, placing his hand on his holster—the real one.

"She tore it up, and I need to redraw it." I place the hair, the ears. I think a nostril is part of the cleft and put it under his chin. "Damn, that's wrong." I look up at the sergeant. "Do you mind if I use your tape?" I don't wait for the answer and pull off a few pieces from the dispenser on the desk. "This is part of his nose for sure, and his mouth goes here, with the cleft underneath . . ." I sigh with frustration. "It was so good, real, alive. It must have looked like him because she went hysterical, crazy wild, and then stopped like a switch turned off, denied everything, and tore it up. Suddenly it *wasn't* him, even though she knew it was, even though she described him to me—everything about him. Damn. And now look at it. A mess. I'm a mess, too. This whole day is a mess."

I'm exhausted, confused, bewildered—and now second-guessing my decision to come here. I feel defeated and sink down onto the chair behind Sergeant Daniels's desk. The short cop, Detective Cole, looks like he wants to pull the chair out from under me.

"Who is 'she'?" Sergeant Daniels asks.

"Willa Pressman, and this face I drew—he's the one who raped her, beat her." I finish taping the scraps of the sketch and mourn the end product. It looks like a Picasso drawing gone bad. "There are some things still recognizable, like the cleft here on his chin, and I guess the shape of his face, his hair." I hold it out to them.

They look at each other as if they were just punk'd.

"I'll redraw for it you, no problem. It won't take me long at all. I'll do anything you want—even put up with the inevitable shit from Willa. We have to catch him—we do!"

Detective Cole snorts. Sergeant Daniels rubs his jaw and decides not to take the sketch from me. "Uh, thank you for your generous offer, but Miss Pressman doesn't remember her attacker."

"She remembers everything," I argue.

"Well, if that's the case, Miss Washington—"

"Bea. I would prefer Bea."

"If that's the case, we'll bring her back in here, in front of our forensic artists, and they'll draw him," Sergeant Daniels says.

"But you don't have to. I already drew him, I know I did—this is him." I stand. "So now you just have to locate him and catch him," I challenge, still holding out the sketch.

Detective Cole chuckles. "Catch him? Hey, little girl, I have an idea . . . why don't you go back to your crack house, or wherever you hang out. We have more important things to do here than chase a Mr. Potato Head drawing." He laughs at his stupid joke.

This pisses me off big time and taps into my inherited Italian fury. "Hey, I'm not a crackhead! I'm sober, have been for over three months now, and I'm damn proud of it!" I snap up my three-month chip from the pile on the desk and toss it to Detective Cole. "You think I would have walked in here if I were using? Are you nuts? And with all due respect, I wasn't the one playing a cops-and-robbers video game a minute ago! I didn't have to come here, believe me. I didn't *want* to come here. I thought I should for once do something responsible in my life and stop another girl from getting hurt. But forget it. You don't care. Nobody cares." I begin to throw all the crap into my bag. "And give me back my chip!" I snatch it from Detective Cole.

Sergeant Daniels pours a cup of coffee and hands it to me. "Detective Cole didn't mean that, did you, Cole?"

His subordinate rolls his eyes.

"Congratulations on your sobriety—that's terrific," the sergeant continues, "and it's great that you want to help. But I need to understand something. Are you friends with Willa Pressman? Is that why you want to help, why you're here?"

Now it's my turn to laugh and almost do a spit-take with the coffee. "Do I look like her type? I mean, come on. Think about it."

"No, no, you don't. Not at all." Detective Cole scoffs.

"So, if you're not her friend, why the concern?" The sergeant's blond, bushy brows furrow together. "Do you know something about this we don't? I mean, besides this sketch?"

I think about the girl in the Arboretum, her voice. *Help me . . . please, help me . . .* But I can't go there with them, not yet—I don't trust them with that information. "No, I don't. Let's just say we have a lot more in common than you'd think, Willa and me."

"Yeah, right." Cole is unconvinced.

"Well," the sergeant interrupts, "like I said, we'll have to get her back in here. Ask her some more questions and talk about this . . . this sketch you drew."

"No! Don't do that," I beg.

"But why not?" the sergeant asks. "I don't understand."

"Because she'll deny it, I told you. She'll deny talking with me, meeting with me. She'll say that this isn't the guy."

"Why would she do that? Why wouldn't she want to identify him if this really is him, as you say?"

"Just because," I hedge.

“Just because *why*?” He doesn’t quit.

“She’ll deny everything because she doesn’t want you to know what really happened, okay? Willa won’t talk to you. She hasn’t told anyone, except for me.” I raise my voice.

“And why is that?” the sergeant asks.

“Because of the truth. Willa is afraid of the truth.”

Sergeant Daniels pauses. He stares at me and squints his green eyes. *The Caribbean*, I think to myself. His eyes are the color of the Caribbean Sea.

. . . Two years ago, Christmas, I was fifteen, and my dad was invited to attend a conference down in Jamaica. It was the first conference Mom wanted to join in on. A happy little family vacation, they imagined, I’m sure.

Well, it didn’t turn out that way, as I immediately zeroed in on another bored teen—a nerd from California. He’d been there a couple weeks and told me that he scored amazing weed from the local maintenance workers. He wasn’t cute and was a bit of a moron, but I decided to hang out with him—for the pot—and got stoned with him on the beach.

Stupid move on my part, because after we got high, he thought I should pay him for the weed. With sex.

I was totally grossed out, said “no way,” and he got pissed—majorly pissed. I tried to run from him, but he was fast, caught up with me, and pulled my hair.

“Fuck you!” I yelled and instinctively elbowed him in

his skinny ribs, and he slumped over. I was surprised—kind of knocked the wind out of him. "Cool," I thought and swung around and punched, undercutting his jaw. He stumbled back, dazed, and I ran into the ocean and started swimming—fast.

I lucked out—apparently the stooge didn't know how to swim, because he stayed on the shore in his tacky board shorts, giving me the finger and swearing stupid shit at me.

I swam to an anchored raft, collapsed on my belly, and stared at the water. It was good weed, he was right. I was mesmerized, paralyzed by the beauty, the clarity, the greenness of the sea. I think I must have zoned out on that raft for a good five hours until my mom discovered where I was and called me to shore. She tended to my outrageously burned skin for the rest of the week.

No, it wasn't a good vacation.

Anyway, that greenness, that clarity is what I see in Sergeant Daniels's eyes.

"And you happen know the truth? What happened that night?" he asks.

"I do."

"How?"

I wonder if I should dare go there—to my truth. I give him a nibble. "I sort of drew it out of her."

Sergeant Daniels raises his eyebrows. "Well, that sounds

like quite a talent, Miss Washington. How do you suppose you were able to do that?"

"Look, that's irrelevant. All that matters is he's out there, the rapist. And he looks like this." I hold up the taped sketch again.

They both laugh this time.

"Well, not like *this*. You know what I mean."

"Okay, okay. We'll see what we can do. Why don't you give me your address and phone number, in case we need to talk to you."

I jot my information on a piece of paper and hand it to Sergeant Daniels. "This was a waste of my time, wasn't it?"

"Listen, you're a sweet kid, trying to help a friend, or whatever she is to you."

"I'm not a kid—I'm almost eighteen. Oh, and by the way, can I have a note for school, you know, explaining why I'm not there?"

The sergeant could have laughed at me, I realized after I replayed that last line in my head. But he didn't. He handed me his card. "Give them this. They can call me if they need to."

• • •

I sit in my trusty Volvo, wondering if I should go to school. It was nice of Sergeant Daniels to give me his card, but I don't know how that'll fly with the front office. Like I'm really going to ask them to call the police to find out where I was? And with how I look right now? Not happening—not going to school.

I am cold, wet, dirty, hungry, and man, do I have to pee.

Why do I care so much? Why am I putting myself in this position for her? For Willa Pressman? Jeopardizing school? Ruining my favorite shoes and losing a fabulous coat?

I think about all the sketchy situations I've put myself in—the dangerous places, the dishonest, abusive people I've confronted—the world of an addict. How have I dodged the bullet?

Luck. Shameful, cowardly luck.

I pull to the side of the road and redraw the sketch of Willa's rapist.

And in black marker, I write on the top:

WANTED RAPIST
(POSSIBLE MURDERER)
CALL 734-555-1289
WITH ANY INFORMATION!!!

Then I pull into a Kinkos and make one hundred copies.

• • •

I run up to my bedroom, collapse on the bed, and pull the covers over my head—and try not to think, not to feel, not to care. Just for an hour, a minute . . . I'd even take one second.

Knock, knock.

My mom opens the door to my room. "Why are you home from school? You okay, Bea?"

I fake a cough. "I have a sore throat."

She sits on my bed, pulls down the comforter, and feels my forehead. "Well, you don't have a fever. But you do look horrible. What's that in your hair?"

"Bird shit . . . don't ask."

"Oh god. Go take a shower."

"I just want to sleep, Mom."

"I'm sure you do, but you have that interview today—at the preschool, remember?"

I put my pillow over my face. "Oh, come on, Mom, please don't make me do that. *Please*."

She removes the pillow. "I know you've been through a lot. But maybe working with kids will be a good distraction, get your mind off what happened."

"I doubt that."

"Bea, I promised the preschool director that you would come. It's a couple of afternoons a week. Now, why don't you go take a shower, and I'll heat up some soup."

"But the sore throat thing, Mom . . . I could get the kids sick."

"Are you kidding me? They're walking petri dishes."

Oh great. Just great.

3 months
8 days
16 hours

I can't believe I'm actually doing this. I've never spent more than a couple minutes—that is, consciously—with a kid, and that didn't turn out too well.

I was hired to babysit my neighbor's eight-year-old about a year ago, and I thought, *How hard could it be? Watching a kid for a couple hours—a few extra bucks.* I turned on a video for him and fell asleep, into a deep sleep. (I was coming down from a high.) He got hungry and couldn't wake me, so he proceeded to make his own dinner. The screeching smoke alarms are what woke me—that, and the smell of burnt macaroni and cheese. The house didn't burn down, no one was hurt, thank goodness, but I was never asked again to babysit—duh—and my mom had to replace the scorched pan.

The perky director of Happy Days preschool greets me with a big smile. "So you're Annabelle's daughter. I'm Eve.

Eve Stuart." She checks me out, seems unconvinced.

"I'm Bea," I say, wondering how much she knows about me, what my mom has told her.

"Don't you love the mural your mom painted? The kids sure do."

The familiar puppy-dog and kitty-cat theme that wraps the walls of my house also wraps the walls in the school. "Sure. It's great. Original," I lie.

"So the actual day for the kids ends at three o'clock. But a few of them stay after until their parents pick them up—can be as late as six. I would need your help keeping an eye on them, playing with them, pushing them on swings"—she eyes my platform shoes—"and helping them in the bathroom."

You're kidding me. Ick.

"Of course, I'll be here the whole time—you'll be assisting me. So, why don't you have a seat with the kids?" She gestures toward a few brats on the floor playing with LEGO blocks. "Let's see how you get along."

"Oh, okay." I sit down on the rug, cursing the low-rise skinny jeans that I decided to wear. It's hard to bend my knees and, for sure, my butt crack is peeking out.

I smile at the kids. "Hi."

They ignore me. I'm not a LEGO piece.

"It's called parallel play," Eve says from across the room. "Start playing along with them, you'll see."

I pick up one of the blocks and connect it to another.

Doesn't seem so hard, so I build a box. A little boy uses my arm as a ramp for the car he has constructed.

"Vroom." He races.

I look at Eve. She smiles, nods, and mouths, "See?"

"What's your name?" the little boy asks, still driving.

"Bea."

He laughs, holding his belly. "Her name is a bee—a bug. Ewww."

A bossy little girl corrects him. "Cameron, a bee is not a bug. It's an insect." She looks at me. "My name is Amanda, and he's Cameron. And you have a funny name, and your hair looks messy, and there are pens sticking out."

"Hi, Amanda. It's nice to meet you, too. And yes, I do have pens in my hair, because I like to draw."

A curly-haired girl plops herself down on my lap. "My name is Maisy, and I like to draw, too. My mom says I'm going to be an artist when I grow up. What do you like to draw?"

I take a piece of paper off a table, pull a pen out of my hair, and draw a picture of a bee.

The kids gasp.

"That looks just like a bee!" Amanda exclaims.

"Yup. That's me! But I don't buzz, and I don't have a stinger," I tease.

The kids giggle.

"Oh, wow, you are an artist!" Maisy looks up at me wide-eyed.

"Thank you, Maisy." I smile.

"But why do you have crazy hair?" Amanda asks.

"I think it's pretty." Maisy pets my hair. "It tickles." She giggles. "Could you draw me a kitten? I wuv kittens."

"Sure I can," I say, drawing.

"Oh, she's so cute. She looks real, like I could pet her," Maisy says. "I like you, Bea."

"I like her, too, Maisy," Amanda adds.

"Now draw the kitten pooping," Cameron blurts out. The girls look disgusted. "And frowing up."

"How old are you, Cameron?" I ask before the kitten has diarrhea.

"I'm four." He stands and pounds his chest.

"We are, too," Amanda calls out. "We're all four."

"How old are you, Bea?" Maisy asks.

"I'm four, too," I joke.

"No, you're not," Cameron protests. "You're lying. It's not nice to lie."

"You're right. I'm not four. I'm four, plus four, plus four, plus four, plus one. I'm seventeen years old."

"Wow. That's a lot of fours. You're old," Cameron says.

The director stands. "Okay, kids, it's time to go outside."

"But we want to stay here with Bea," Maisy pouts.

"Not right now, Maisy," the director says. "But maybe Bea will come back here and play with us?" She smiles at me and asks, "You think you could?"

It wasn't as bad as I thought. "Sure, Maisy. I'll see you in a couple days, okay?"

Maisy hugs me around the neck and whispers in my ear, "I want to be just like you when I get all growed up."

I hug her back. *Oh, no, you don't, honey. No, you don't.*

3 months 9 days 8 hours

It's Tuesday morning, and I trudge through the halls of Packard High. Chris is waiting for me at my locker. He looks anxious, flushed.

"Bea! Where were you yesterday? And why didn't you answer your phone? Willa is spreading vicious rumors about you."

I unlock my locker. "Sore throat in the morning, had to work at that preschool in the afternoon, AA at night. I'm beat."

"Willa is telling everyone that you're a slut—that you slept with everybody and anybody for drugs!"

"Uh-huh, what else?" I pull my books out.

"That you tested positive for HIV and want to infect the whole school."

I laugh. "Gotta hand it to her . . . that's a good one."

"Wait, it gets better"—he laughs now, too—"you've been practicing witchcraft for a while, and you've made a voodoo doll of her and pierce her every night with needles!"

"I've always wanted to be a Wiccan!" I slam my locker shut.

"Seriously, how did you manage to piss her off so much? What did you do?"

"I drew the truth out of her."

"Oh, shit. Does this have something to do with"—he looks around and whispers—"your power?"

"Maybe."

"You're not using again, right, like she says?"

"Believe me, I'm not using. I'd be in a better mood if I were." I sink my back against the cold metal door. "She told me, Chris—everything that happened that night. It was horrible, so horrible." I show him the stack of flyers tucked away in my bag. "And this is the guy, the rapist."

"Why would she do that? Tell you what happened?"

"Because she's scared and she wants help. She *needs* help. And I'm the only one around here who sees the lie she's been living, the only one who hasn't been suckered into her fantasy life."

"What are you talking about? She's, like, perfect. Willa Pressman has never done anything wrong."

I sigh. The bell rings, I look around at the walking dead in the halls, and decide to write down the mind-blowing words to Chris.

Willa is a drug addict!

He reads, slams my book shut, and shoos his hands at me like I'm a pesky gnat. "Bea, come on, get real. Did you draw that? *See* that?"

"I didn't have to. It's like a secret language we have. Look, Chris, it's okay if you don't get it."

"What are you planning on doing with those flyers?"

"I'm going to paper them around town after school, in stores, restaurants, bowling alleys—anywhere I can. I mean, what do I have to lose? My reputation?" I look at him and smile. "Wouldn't mind a little company."

"I don't know. I have the gay/straight alliance club at four today."

"Whatever. I don't blame you."

"It's not that I don't want to help you . . ."

The bell rings.

"Let's go. We can't be late for art class. I think it's 'how to draw a stick figure' today," I joke.

• • •

"Today is movie day," Mrs. Hogan announces. The class, listening for once, applauds her decision. "We'll be watching the classic film *Lust for Life*." Some of the students snicker. "No, it's not about that, it's about the famous painter Vincent van Gogh." She pronounces "Gogh" like *gog*, with a hard *g*.

Chris rolls his eyes at me.

A sleepy stoner takes a pack of cigarettes from the side pocket of his backpack—doesn't even attempt to hide them. "Ah, Mrs. Hogan? Could I be excused? I have to go to the john."

"Fine, make sure you take the pass hanging on the board. But ten minutes, that's it. And be quiet when you come back in. You don't want to interrupt the movie."

Willa raises her hand. "Mrs. Hogan, can I also have a pass to use the ladies' room?"

The teacher's head shoots up. "Of course. Do you need help?"

"No, no, thank you, I'm fine." Willa walks toward the door.

"Take your time, Willa. All the time you need."

Willa leaves the room, and Mrs. Hogan turns off the lights and closes the shades.

The movie begins, and in the darkness, I find myself nodding off, falling into the swirls of van Gogh's paint strokes. I drift away into his starry night, into the vibrant palette of golds, greens, and blues, and my head falls to my chest, dreaming about the colors of her dress, my mom's dress . . .

. . . a vibrant, flowing dress. She was beautiful, barefoot, her hair loose.

My parents were having a party in our Chicago apartment. I was four, maybe five, sitting above, watching the whole scene from my railed-off loft bed. Mom was dancing, flitting around friends, sipping at an open bottle of champagne. She looked so happy.

The loft was filled with oils, half-painted canvases, charcoal nudes covering the tall white walls.

Dad was across the room, eying my mom, watching her. He didn't look as happy as she did.

Mom opened the sliding glass door to the terrace and tripped, spilled champagne, laughed at herself, and then closed the door behind her. My dad, looking bothered, walked toward the terrace. He opened the door, and I smelled the sweet, smoky scent of . . .

. . . pot as the stoner floats back into the classroom. The smell awakens me.

Willa comes in shortly after. *Maybe she's found a replacement for Marcus.*

She walks in the darkness, trips on something, and takes hold of the back of my chair.

I whisper, "You okay?"

Willa falls, crumbling to the ground, and wails, "Oh my gosh, you tripped me!"

The lights flip on, and Mrs. Hogan stops the movie. "What happened? What happened, Willa?"

Willa holds her right knee and points at me. "That new girl. She tripped me. Ow. It hurts, my knee."

I look around the room in defense, not knowing what to do or say. "I didn't trip you, Willa. I didn't. I just asked if you were okay."

Willa gasps. "You've been so mean to me, ever since you

came to this school. Why do you have to be so mean? What did I ever do to you, anyway?"

"I'm not mean to you, Willa. In fact, I think it's the other way around, what you've been saying about me."

"Did you hear that?" Willa howls. "She tripped me and won't even admit it. She's been stalking me, talking crap about me. Lying. Saying horrible, just horrible things about me, Mrs. Hogan!" Willa pretends to sob.

"I am not. And I didn't trip her." I look to Chris for help.

"Mrs. Hogan," Chris tries to come to my rescue. "There's no way Bea would have tripped her, no way."

"Stay out of this, Chris," Mrs. Hogan orders and helps Willa off the ground, walking her to her desk. She scratches off a note and hands it to me. "Beatrice, you are to go directly to Principal Nathanson's office. He'll know how to handle this situation."

I hold the note in my hand. "You're kidding me, right? I have to go to the principal's office? I don't even know where his office is."

"Now!" she barks.

I look at Chris. He mouths the words "I'm sorry."

I rise. And as I leave the room, I look at Willa. She shoots me a wry, crooked smile.

• • •

Swallowed up in a gigantic, brown pleather chair, I sit in Principal Nathanson's office, doodling in my book, waiting for him to finish up an important phone call dealing with a football player and his failing grades. He looks like a rat: beady eyes, ugly teeth, chomping away at the phone.

His glasses keep sliding off his sweaty nose, and he pushes them up with his middle finger like he's saying "Screw you" to me over and over. He finally finishes up the phone call, conceding, "I'll make sure the D is raised to a C."

He hangs up the phone and looks at me. "Well, well, well," he stalls. He has no idea who I am, why I am here.

An image surges through my head—*oh crap, he's thinking of my breasts, my cleavage . . . I don't want to know what else!*

I tuck my pen in my hair, close my book, pull my sweater up, and sit on my hands.

The creep!

He sighs, reading the note from Mrs. Hogan. His fat lips move as he reads; spittle forms at the corner of his mouth. "Oh, dear," he mutters, then looks up at me and gives me the finger again. "You tripped her? Willa Pressman?"

"She said I did, but I didn't. She tripped on something and grabbed my chair for balance. I asked her if she was okay, and she threw herself on the ground, got hysterical, and accused me. That's what happened."

Principal Nathanson clucks his tongue. "How could you be so insensitive? Tripping her like that?"

"But I *didn't*."

"And this note says you've been making up lies about her. After all she's been through?" He pulls up my file on his computer screen. "If I recall correctly, didn't we take you into this school as a last resort? Quite a generous gesture, I would add, given all your"—he reads—"issues."

"I didn't trip her. And I haven't been harassing her or making things up." I try again.

"She says you have."

"And of course, you believe her word over mine," I resign.

"Miss Washington"—he stands, pacing behind his desk—"Willa has been at our school since the seventh grade. She's been a model student—outstanding, even. She's from a well-respected family. You, however, have been here, what, a week? I know nothing about you or your family. Tell me, why *wouldn't* I believe Willa over you?"

I almost laugh. Willa is good—better than I ever was with the deceit. She has everyone fooled. There's not one person in this moronic school who knows Willa for who she really is.

I realize it's time to wave the white flag and continue on with my crappy day—fake it till you make it—and get back to art class to watch the end of Mr. van *Gog*. "I'm sorry, Mr. Nathanson. It won't happen again. I promise."

The principal looks surprised at my apology and swallows. His big, ugly Adam's apple travels up and down his neck. I guess he's not used to student remorse. He gives me the finger once again as he pushes his glasses up his nose. "Well, that's fine for now. But if I hear about any other shenanigans from you, I'll have to involve your parents, you understand?"

"Please, there's no need to call them." *God forbid.* "I

promise you, no more shenanigans from me. Never."

"Well, I'm glad we had this little chat, uh"—he looks down at my file, clearly searching for my first name—"Brenda."

I don't feel the need to correct him—let me be a Brenda, that's fine. Brenda, I'm sure, doesn't get into as much trouble as I do and probably has straight hair. "I am, too, Mr. Nathanson."

"You know, we have a counselor here, if you ever need to talk about things."

Mrs. Hogan. The teacher who sent me here in the first place.

He opens the door, signaling that it's time for me to get the hell out.

I push myself up and out of the super-sized chair. He stares at my breasts again, catches himself, scratches the inside of his ear, and takes a look at his finger, like something important came out of it.

Perv.

3 months
9 days
15.5 hours

Thankfully this long, extremely unpleasant day at school has ended, and I'm at my car, prepared to paper the town, when I notice a note tucked under my windshield wiper.

> Hey, DRUGGIE STALKER FREAK, you'd better not say shit to anybody—nobody—or I'll take you down, hard.

And she keyed my car! A foot-long scrape is etched along the driver's-side door.

Shit.

"Bea! Bea!" Chris runs up to me, out of breath. "I'm coming with you!"

"You changed your mind?"

"I'm sorry I didn't help you out in art class."

"It's not your fault. Everyone believes every word she says."

"I don't. I believe you. I do."

I smile at my buddy. "Okay, you sure you're alright with this? Because I'm not so sure anymore." I show him the note, the scratch.

"Oh, man. That sucks."

"Yeah, it does."

"Come on, let's go." Chris jumps in my car.

"I have to call my mom first—gotta keep her chill. She's so spooked!"

"She and me both."

I dial her number and hear the tinkling of ice in a glass before she says, "Hello?"

"Hi, Mom, just wanted you to know that I'm going to hang out with Chris for a couple hours, get a bite with him."

I listen.

"You what? Oh come on, Mom. You're kidding, right?" I hand the phone to Chris. "She wants to talk to you."

Chris points to himself and mouths "Me?"

I nod.

"Um, hi . . . um, Mrs. Washington"—he gulps—"yeah, sure." He listens. "Uh huh, yeah, that would be nice." He whispers to me, "She invited me over for dinner sometime."

I snatch the phone away from him. "Okay, you cool now, Mom? I'll keep in touch. Bye." I hang up.

"And you said yes?" I scold Chris.

"What was I supposed to say? And what's the problem, anyway? I think it's nice."

"You don't want to come to my house. It's weird, they're weird—and the food is horrible."

"Speaking of food, I'm hungry. Feel like a burger?"

"We have important work to do first. I tell you what. Let's put in an hour of posting the flyers, and I'll buy you a burger—my treat."

"Deal."

We start in a hip historic area in downtown Ann Arbor, Kerrytown, loaded with awesome shops that I *so* can't afford; trendy restaurants; art galleries with bad, overpriced art; and out-of my-league antique stores. Shoppers, students, tourists stroll the tree-lined streets.

We make a good team—walking in and out of buildings, looking for the official police sketch. Once spotted, I yank down the flyer, and Chris, carrying the staple gun, quickly tacks up the new sketch.

I approach a woman in a navy peacoat at the bustling farmers market. "Excuse me. Does this man look familiar to you?" I show her the flyer.

She ignores me, filling a paper bag with McIntosh apples.

"Maybe you could take it with you?" I hand it to her. "You could ask your friends if they've seen him, if they recognize him. It'd be so helpful."

"Sure," she agrees and walks away from the apple stand.

I watch her throw the flyer in the first trash can she passes.

"Oh, come on!" I dive into the trash and retrieve the flyer. "No one cares, Chris. I'm sure they think I'm just another crazy college student with a cause."

He ignores my rant. "Great, now you're digging in the garbage. It's been over an hour. You promised. I'm tired and super hungry."

"Okay, okay, burger time."

Chris and I nudge our way into University Tavern, a crowded student hangout that happens to serve *the best burgers in southern Michigan*, the sign outside brags.

And I'm hit. Hard.

Slammed with the smells and sounds of *fun*: laughter marinated in booze, clinking glasses filled with yeasty beer and wine, stories and secrets whispered, laughed, and shared over goblets and mugs. I immediately resent my enforced sobriety and sense the foreboding, revved-up semi-truck barreling toward me.

It's not fair! How can they all have so much fun, and I can't?

Chris and I stand, squeezed in with damp-smelling people waiting for a table. I crack my knuckles, my neck, my toes. Beads of sweat dampen the back of my sweater. I check my phone for messages from my nonexistent friends.

"You okay?" Chris pokes me. "There's a lot of partying going on here."

"Yeah, fools." I loosen my scarf and then snatch the stapler from Chris. I feel the urge to staple everyone's hands to the shiny, lacquered wood bar. *Cha-chink. Cha-chink. Cha-chink. Cha-chink . . . fuck you fools! You can't have a drink!*

But instead I push my way through the crowd to the front bulletin corkboard.

"Excuse me," I say to a stupid guy with an ugly dark beard blocking the board. I try to shove past him. My hair gets caught in one of his top coat buttons. "Ow! Fuck! That hurts!"

"Sorry," he lamely says, as his fingers detangle the knot.

"Whatever." I scratch my head and staple the flyer to the board, not once, twice, but eight friggin' times—fantasizing the whole time that they're the hands holding the drinks that *I can't*.

"Bea!" Chris calls out. "We got a table. Come on!"

The waitress weaves us through the crowd, and we collapse into a cracked red vinyl booth and say in unison, "Two burgers with everything on it and a couple Diet Cokes."

"Jinx." Again, said in unison.

I pull off my coat and spot a guy with a "you really should wash your hair now and then, but it's still sexy" kind of look, smiling at me in the next booth, kitty-corner from us. He's with another dude, and they're drinking a pitcher of beer and slopping down a pizza.

I smile back, sort of. My smile still feels like it's not quite working at full capacity yet with the opposite sex; it's jerky, like it needs a squirt of oil or something.

I lean forward and whisper to Chris, "Check it out: seven o'clock, your time."

Chris casually removes his coat, looks over his shoulder, and reports back. "Meh. Not my type."

"Really? You don't think he's hot?"

"He looks like a bro."

"I don't know." I finger a strand of frizz hanging down my face. "This whole flirting, hooking-up thing. I've been out of it for a while."

"As you should be. Do you really want to complicate your life any more?"

I jiggle my legs under the table. "Yeah. I do." I smile again at the guy, a little more confidently this time. "Hi."

He says "hi" back. "I'm Malcolm. He's Eric."

Chris kicks me.

Ouch. "I'm Bea."

The waitress sets our burgers and pop on the table.

"Bea, I have to go to the little boy's room—be back in a sec. Stay out of trouble." Chris gestures with his head toward Malcolm's table. "Okay, promise?"

"Of course." I shoo him off, already pulling a flyer out of my bag.

Chris walks away, and I hand the sketch to Malcolm. "Hey. You wouldn't happen to recognize this guy, would you?"

Malcolm and Eric mull it over, whisper to each other.

"What do you think?" I ask. "Look familiar to you?"

"Oh man, it's strange." Malcolm scratches his dirty hair. "I think we may know him, a guy named Winston."

Eric snaps his fingers. "Yeah, Winston, right. The eyes, a little bit. And the chin thing for sure. Weird."

"Really? You sure?"

"Join us." Malcolm pats the seat next to him.

"Okay."

He scootches over, and I sit. He smells like a clump of wet clay for some reason—it's not a particularly bad smell, not good either, just clayish. "So, Winston? That's his name?"

"Yeah, he's that loner dude, right?" Malcolm jabs Eric.

Eric nods. "Always alone. Doesn't talk much." He leans forward and whispers, "The rumor is that he catches rodents around campus and brings them up to his dorm room like they're his pets."

"And I heard that he tortures them and decapitates them," Malcolm adds.

I shiver. "That's horrible."

"I know, right? Damn, where are my manners?" Malcolm tops off his glass of beer from the pitcher and hands it to me.

"Thanks, but I have a Coke."

"Come on, you look a little stressed."

"Well, I am sort of, yeah."

Eric holds up his glass. "Cheers."

I stare hard at the beer and lick my lips. *What would a little sip hurt, anyway? No one would know. It's not like I'd go out using again—a little buzz, what's the harm? It's just a beer, not a semi-truck coming at me—more like a flat-tired pickup. It wouldn't show up on a test.*

I hold the cold glass dripping with condensation and bring it to my lips. The frothy foam at the top tickles my nose and my belly—sends a zingy feeling up from my gut to my head. A head so tired of being filled with people's shit. *Yes. Fill me up with something else, please!*

Slap! The glass flies out of my hand, splashing my fantasy all over the table and onto Malcolm and Eric's laps.

"Bea!" Chris stands above me. "What are you doing?"

Malcolm and Eric jump up, their jeans soaked with beer. "You dick! What's your problem, faggot?"

"Hey," I yell at Malcolm. "He's my friend! You can't talk to him like that!"

"We're going home! Now, Bea!" Chris pulls me up from the booth.

"Chris, I know they're jerks, but they know who the rapist is! His name is Winston and he's a loner and captures rodents on campus, brings them up to his dorm room, makes them his pets, and he tortures them, decapitates them, and, oh no . . ." As soon as the words come out of my mouth, I get the joke. I've been duped. They made the whole thing up.

I'm *so* the fool.

Malcolm and Eric grab a pile of napkins from a dispenser and wipe up the mess, continuing to razz me. "Yeah, and he holds satanic rituals in the Science Quad every full moon and runs naked through the campus on the first Monday of every month." Malcolm snorts. "You and Winston will make a great couple!"

Chris wraps up our burgers, throws some money on the table, and drags me out of the tavern.

We pass the corkboard. "Shit, look! Someone took down the flyer already!"

Chris pushes me out the door.

He drives my car and delivers a well-deserved verbal spanking. "What were you thinking? Why would you give it all up, all the months you have, for those assholes and a lousy beer?"

"I don't know. I just don't know." I light up a cigarette, open the window. "I feel like I'm on a Ferris wheel of confusion that doesn't stop. Just when I think I can step out, it flies up to the top again and dangles, swaying back and forth. I think about it every day—using. Every day."

Chris pulls my car into his driveway and parks. "Bea, you should give it a rest—this Willa thing. It's stressing you out too much. She isn't worth it."

"It isn't just about Willa." I pinch my nose between my eyes, hoping the tears don't start up again. "That girl in Ann Arbor—the girl found dead last week. She was my best friend at Athena Day. Her name was Aggie."

"What? Oh, Bea. Why didn't you tell me?"

"I saw her that night. I was one of the last people to see her. I could have helped her." My eyes burn with shameful tears.

Chris reaches out, cups the back of my neck.

"I can't seem to help anyone, Chris." I look out the window and blow out a trail of smoke. "Not Willa, not even myself. It's so hard, so damn hard."

Chris takes the cigarette out of my hand. He inhales, coughs, gags, and sputters, "Ick. Ugh."

I pat him on his back. "Jesus, what are you doing?"

"I just wish I knew what you were going through," he says through coughs. "How hard it must be. Maybe, somehow, I could help you then."

"Thanks, Chris, but you can't. And I don't think getting sick on a cigarette will do either of us any good."

"Bea, maybe you don't see yourself the way I see you, but you're fighting the fight. Every day, every hour, every minute. It's the fire in your eyes these days—different from last winter at camp. It's raw, real, and yes, pained. Maybe the Ferris wheel isn't letting you off today, but it will. Or maybe being up in the sky, looking down, is exactly where you need to be right now."

"Are you kidding me?" I take the cigarette back from him. "When did you get to be so smart?"

"The moment I knew for sure that I was gay. Fifteen. And no, the ride didn't stop; it just continued around and around, picking up speed. I thought I was mad until I realized one day, whoa, I'm in control, no one else. I'm not the one on the Ferris wheel, it's the people around me who are spinning. Not me. I'm grounded. I know who I am."

I'm silenced by his insight.

Ping. I get a text and read:

spotted winston howling at the moon tonite. i think he's coming to get u. —malcolm

"Oh, shit." I show it to Chris.

"They have your number from the flyer!"

I can't help but laugh. "Oh, damn, they do. They really were assholes, weren't they?"

Chris laughs with me. "Big-time assholes."

"I can't believe I fell for it. Thanks for protecting me."

Chris takes my hand, wraps his fingers around mine. "You would've done the same for me. You were ready to take on a two-hundred-pound fullback, remember?"

"I do, yeah." I squeeze and look at his hand. "Let go of me, Chris."

"Excuse me?"

I open my sketchbook and turn to a clean page. "I just figured out how you can help. Put your left hand down on the paper." He does. I trace it.

"It tickles."

"Okay. Lift up." Chris moves his hand, and I place my left hand down and trace inside his, crossing the lines. "There. My hand will always be in yours."

• • •

I drive by Aggie's house on my way home from Chris's.

The gate is open, and cars fill the expansive drive. I park across the street from the massive house and look through the front living room window. They must be "sitting shivah," where friends and family visit and mourn for seven days—it's a Jewish tradition. I see dozens of people—girls from Athena Day, relatives, Aggie's mom and dad.

I should be there. I was closer to her than anybody.

The side door of the house opens. Maria, their housekeeper, walks out to the trash cans with a bag of garbage. I jump out of my car. "Maria!" I call out.

She drops the bag and crosses the street, rushing toward me. Maria crushes my ribs with her hug; her short, taut body heaves with sobs.

"Beatrice, my Beatrice. I'm so glad you are here."

"I feel so bad, Maria." I cry, too.

"I know, baby, I know." She wipes her eyes with a dish towel that's buttoned to her apron and takes my face in her hands—studies my eyes, pets my hair. "Are you alright, Beatrice? Are you doing okay? Tell me the truth."

I nod. "I am, Maria. I've been clean for over three months," I say through a knotted throat.

Maria makes the sign of the cross. "Oh, thank you, thank you god for that." Her strong hands take hold of mine. "Promise me something, please."

"I promise."

"Promise me that you will never, ever think that you

are at fault. Do you hear me? I do not blame you. No one should blame you."

Tears roll down my cheeks.

"I knew what was going on with Agatha, you know that, right? I wanted to help her."

"I know you did."

"I've been with Agatha since she was a baby. I know what she did—what she did to you, to others. But they"—she looks back at the house—"refused to believe it. It wasn't on their agenda, wasn't convenient for them to know the truth. So I did nothing. I was instructed to do nothing, even when I brought up my concerns. My poor, poor Agatha."

"Maybe I could have—"

Maria covers my mouth with her hand. "No, you couldn't have. Nobody could have. You are a good girl, Beatrice. Always were—I saw it in your soul, your eyes, how caring, how loving a friend you were."

I smile. "I'd better go. It's getting late, and I don't want to worry my parents."

She takes a deep breath and wipes my tears. "I'm so proud of you, Beatrice Francesca. Okay, you go on now. I will pray for you."

"Thank you. Thank you, Maria."

• • •

The texts continue while I get ready for bed:

malcolm gave me your # hook up? winston wants to watch 2. lol —dan

heard u give out. call me. —jock's trap

frat party tomorrow nite—winstons gonna b there with a couple rats —manny

winston's smoking hot, baby —malcolm

check out woolf on campus. hes your guy. —J.W.

he vants to suck your blood —malcolm

My cell continues to ping with messages, so I throw it across the room. It bounces off my closet door, and I immediately regret it, hoping the phone didn't break.

Damn!

I pick it up, and a photograph begins to download, sent by Malcolm—an obscene photo of his "shortcomings."

Gross.

I turn it off, fall into bed, and pull the covers up and over my head. Force myself to sleep.

3 months 10 days 7 hours

Worst sound in the world? Hands down, it's the alarm clock buzzing, screaming at me at seven to drag my butt out of bed.

I slam down the button, fall back on my warm-with-sleep, comfy pillow, and yawn. And then the events of yesterday come crashing into my consciousness.

Oh, shit.

I take my cell off the nightstand, turn it on, and brace myself for the anticipated onslaught of obscene frat-boy messages. The screen lights up, ripe with ridicule, I'm sure.

10 TEXT MESSAGES!

1 VOICE MAIL!

I hit voice mail—seems the safest choice.

"Miss Washington? This is Sergeant Daniels. We need you to come into the station immediately."

I throw my arms up in the air. "What did I do now? Sheesh!"

My phone rings in my hand. I answer. "Hello?"

"Do you want me to pick you up? I'm in the neighborhood."

"Sergeant Daniels, is that you?"

"Yes. I need you in my office ASAP."

"Okay, okay . . . no, don't come over here, please. My parents will flip out. I have study hall first period today—I can miss it, I guess. I'll be there within the hour."

• • •

When I walk into the police station, there she is, standing at the metal detector. I was hoping I'd see her this morning.

Although I didn't have as much time as I wanted, I did dress with her in mind. I left most of my jewelry on my dresser and settled for simple hoop earrings and only a few bangles.

"Good morning." I smile.

She grunts.

My hair is as smooth as it can be—less tangled and frizzy, and bird poop–free. I'm wearing a faux fur cropped jacket, two functional shoes, and I'm clean. I hand her my purse, a vintage Chanel bucket bag, and take off my jacket, revealing a beaded turquoise cardigan over a long, black cotton tee and black leggings. I know I look a lot better than I did when she last saw me.

I take the bangles off my wrists, and the nose ring? Still in my nose, but we both know the wand thingy works.

I pass through security in record time.

I move on to Mr. Toad, who is sleeping, snoring—having a good dream, given the smug smile on his face. I reach around his desk, snatch a couple lollipops from his stash, throw a purple one to the female cop, and keep the orange one for myself.

I score a smile from her.

Sergeant Daniels is on the phone when I enter his office. He has his back to me and is holding what looks like all one hundred of my flyers in his hand.

"You took those down?" I exclaim. "Damn. Do you know how many hours I spent putting them up?"

The sergeant turns, facing me. He looks pissed off, ready to rail, but pauses, hangs up the phone, checks me out, and rubs his brow. "You shouldn't have done that, Miss Washington."

Detective Cole, oblivious of my transformation, has his hand on his holster again, a bad habit of his. "You've tampered with police business, taking down our posters and putting your crazy sketch up. We could have you arrested! You know that?"

"Easy there, Cole . . ." Sergeant Daniels disarms him and looks at me. "Miss Washington—"

"Bea," I say.

"We're going to let this one slide—this tampering business."

Detective Cole sighs.

"*If*, and only *if*, you promise to leave things alone and stop this obsession over the Pressman case," he orders.

"You should be the one obsessed! There's a maniac out there who raped and beat up a seventeen-year-old girl a couple weeks ago. You don't think he's going to do it again to somebody else? Maybe he already has. Who knows? He could be the same guy who attacked the girl in the Arboretum last spring."

"What do you know about that?" Detective Cole demands.

"Everyone knows about her, what happened. It was in all the papers. There has to be a connection. Don't tell me you haven't thought about that. They were both blindfolded, strangled, and raped, right?"

Sergeant Daniels squints his eyes. "How do you know about Willa, how she was when found? We haven't released that information yet."

"She told me."

Detective Cole laughs. "That's funny, because we had Willa back in here, and she said she told you nothing."

"Then I guess I'm psychic, right?" I slither up to him. "Or maybe the more plausible explanation is that she's lying. Have you ever thought of that?"

"Or maybe *you* are," he tosses back.

Sergeant Daniels cuts in. "We're exploring everything we have, Miss Washington—we've got it handled."

"Bea, the name's Bea. And the flyer I've been tacking up

all over town, the flyer that you took down, is a sketch of the rapist. Yeah, sure, that's handling it."

Sergeant Daniels clenches his jaw at my sarcasm.

"Miss Pressman also said you're stalking her and making up stories, says you're a real nutcase at school," Detective Cole spits.

I laugh. "Of course she's saying that. Don't you understand? She doesn't want you to catch him."

"But why would she *not* want us to catch him?" the sergeant asks. "That makes absolutely no sense."

I take a big breath. "Willa Pressman isn't exactly who you think she is. She has a, um . . . a problem."

"Yeah, you!" Detective Cole jumps in.

I'm beginning to hate this guy. But I really don't want to be arrested for accosting an officer, so I take a breath and ask in a nice voice, "Sergeant Daniels, do you think we could talk alone? For a minute?"

The sergeant looks at Detective Cole and gestures with his head for him to leave.

Cole objects. "Oh come on, are you serious? You're not going to believe anything this . . . this *lunatic* utters, are you?"

"Now!" Sergeant Daniels orders.

Detective Cole leaves, stuffing his hands in his pockets like a punished bully on a playground.

We both let out a sigh of relief.

Sergeant Daniels scratches his nose and says under his breath, "Um, by the way, I happened to notice—you look nice, better than the last time I saw you."

"Yeah, well, this is how I normally look. Thanks, though. Do you mind if I sit?"

"Go ahead."

I sit down on a beige upholstered chair in the corner of his office. Sergeant Daniels pulls his desk chair up to me, across from me, and leans forward on his knees.

"So, what's this problem that Miss Pressman has?"

"This is *so* not my business."

"What's not your business?"

"Willa is struggling, really struggling with, well, let's say *stuff*."

"Stuff?"

"Yeah, drugs and stuff."

"Drugs? Willa involved with drugs?" he asks, confused. "That doesn't make sense. She's not that type."

"Type? Ha!" I laugh. "You ought to come to a meeting with me sometime. There's no type. It's everybody, all types."

"Okay, okay . . . again, how do you know this?"

"Because she told me everything! I already explained that to you. She was loaded that night, and he knew it. She had him buy her booze. She joined him in his car willingly. She thinks it was her fault. And she's afraid. Afraid of disappointing her parents, her friends, the school. But her biggest fear? She's afraid of giving up her best friend."

"That being drugs?" he asks.

I nod. "I know. I've been there. It's scary—it's *still* scary."

The sergeant strokes the blond stubble on his chin. "I don't know. This doesn't make sense."

"What is it going to take for you to believe me?"

A faint knock on the door. The sergeant shouts, "Not yet, Cole . . . give us a minute."

But it isn't Detective Cole who enters. A brunette with a pug nose and pouty lips charges into the office carrying a Gucci tote bag. She drops it on his desk, straightens up some of his papers, and places her hands on her hips.

"Betsy." Sergeant Daniels stands.

"Sorry to bother you, but I'm leaving for that conference tomorrow, and I have to go over Max's schedule with you." She looks at me. "This will only take a minute."

She can't be his wife—he doesn't wear a wedding ring and neither does she, and they don't look too happy to see each other. Must be Sergeant Daniels's ex, I bet high school sweethearts, and Max is their son. Huh. He looks too young to have a kid. Must have been a teenage pregnancy, shotgun wedding, quickie divorce.

I pull out my sketchbook.

She reads from a list. "Okay, so Max has his checkup tomorrow morning. Don't be late, or you'll get bumped and you'll be sitting in that office all morning. His piano lesson is after school, and if you have time, the barber is right across the street—it'd be great if he could trim Max's hair. It's looking pretty shaggy, and it's hanging in his eyes. And please rub sunblock on him before baseball practice on Saturday. He's getting self-conscious about his freckles—I guess a couple kids teased him about them at practice, and you know he's not hitting the ball off the tee and sure doesn't need any more teasing. Oh, and *please* do not feed him junk all weekend. He's looking a little pudgy to me. You got all that?"

Sergeant Daniels nods, looks like his tail is between his legs.

"Yes, Betsy. Everything will be fine. Don't worry."

"Sorry again," Betsy says to me. "Cute purse. Bye." She gives us a little wave and closes the door.

The sergeant walks back to me, red-faced. "Now where were we?"

"Here." I rip a page out of my sketchbook. "Does this look like your son, Max?"

He stares at the sketch, then at me, rubs his eyes. "Wait a sec . . . how did you do this?"

He rushes to his desk and searches under papers, pulls out drawers, and holds up a five-by-seven school photograph of his son Max.

Holy crap. I have to admit, I nailed him.

"Did you see this? When you were sitting here, did you see this picture of him?"

"Right." I nod. "While Detective Cole was standing over me, with his hand on his holster, I pilfered through your desk drawers. That makes a lot of sense."

"Then how did you know? How did you know what he looked like?"

"I don't know. Your wife—"

"My ex."

"Your ex-wife described him, and I guess I'm a good listener."

He starts pacing, holding the photo in one hand and my sketch in the other. "This is uncanny. She didn't mention that he wore glasses. She didn't mention anything about glasses, did she?"

"She didn't? Well, she said he couldn't see the ball on the tee, so I assumed he took them off for practice."

"And his dimples . . . you gave him dimples."

"Well, I figured since you have dimples, and your wife does, too."

"Ex."

"Right. Ex. Since she also has dimples . . ."

Sergeant Daniels stops pacing and stares at me, *through* me. And it's not a good stare—it's unnerving. "How did you do this?"

"I don't know, Sergeant. I don't. I've been trying to tell you that. It happens sometimes when I draw. And it's not fun, believe me. I wish it would go away and never come back. Maybe I should stop drawing altogether, like my dad did and throw away the pens, my sketchbook." I look at the wall clock. "Crap, I have to get to school, like five minutes ago. Are we done?"

He doesn't answer me, so I gather up my stuff and rush out of his office with him still staring, open-mouthed, fingering the sketch of his son.

3 months
10 days
16 hours

Maisy comes running up to me, her legs flying, barely touching the ground. "She's back! Bea's back!" She leaps into my arms.

"Hey, Maisy. How are you doing?" I kiss the top of her head.

Cameron and Amanda wave from the sandbox. "Are you going to draw something for us today?" Amanda asks.

"I sure hope it's something pooping." Cameron snorts.

"Hi, Bea!" Eve greets me, smiling. "I have some paperwork I have to do. Will you stay out here with the kids for a bit?"

"Sure. Who wants to swing?"

"I do!" they yell in unison, running downhill to the swing set.

I join them, skipping. "How am I going to push all three of you at once? I only have two hands."

"Well, I know how to pump, so I don't need pushing!" Cameron hops on the highest swing.

"So what, Cameron? I know how to whistle, and you don't." Amanda sticks out her tongue.

"I wish I could whistle." Maisy struggles, climbing onto a swing.

"I can teach you, Maisy. Just like my dad taught me when I was about your age," I say.

"You will? Can you?"

"Of course." I bend down in front of the swing, eye level with Maisy. "Okay, put your lips together and pucker up, like you want a kiss."

Maisy puckers—an exaggerated pucker.

"Okay, now blow!"

She blows through her lips, spit flies, her curls flop forward, and she almost falls off the swing.

"Whoops." I catch her.

"Listen to me!" Amanda performs a perfect whistle.

"That's beautiful, Amanda!"

"Yeah, well, look how high I got!" Cameron yells, flying on his swing.

Maisy pouts.

I give her a little push on the swing. "Don't worry. You keep practicing, and one day you'll be whistling and won't even realize it."

"You promise? Is that what happened to you?"

"Uh-huh. It did."

"When? When did it happen?"

"I think I was about five."

"How? How did you do it?"

"Well, I remember that I was with my dad, and he was drawing . . ."

. . . hunched at a table in our downtown Chicago loft, absorbed, sketching an abstract charcoal drawing and whistling.

Mom was painting on a canvas and started mimicking my dad's whistles, answering him like a bird. They exchanged looks, smiled.

I sat on a futon across from them, my feet tucked under my body, with my own pad of paper on my lap, drawing a pretty picture of my mom with a purple crayon. I wanted to join them, whistling. I tried over and over, but only air came out.

I put my paper and crayon down and walked up to my dad. "Daddy? I keep practicing and practicing. But it's not working."

"What's not working?"

"My whistle. I can't do it like you and Mommy!"

Mom laughed. "Oh, baby, you will, you will."

My dad wiped his hands on a rag and sat me on his lap. "Okay, try again. Put your lips together and pucker up like you want a kiss."

I did, and he kissed me.

"That's not what I want, Daddy!" I pulled back. "I want to whistle!"

"Okay, okay." He smiled. "Now open your lips a little bit, put your tongue on the roof of your mouth, and blow."

I blew as hard as I could. My tight braids swung in front of my face, and I got dizzy. No whistle.

I started to cry, so he scooped me up high in the air and put me on his shoulders. I held on tight to his nappy fro, and he ran all around the loft like an airplane in flight.

"Be careful, Richard." My mom watched us, laughing.

I giggled. "It's really high up here. I wish I were as tall as you."

"You're only five, Bea. Don't worry, you're going to get a lot taller." He plopped me down on the futon. My mom joined us and tickled me.

"What's that you're drawing?" my dad asked, looking at the pad of paper.

"That's Mommy." I showed him. "But I didn't do her face good. She's prettier than this."

"I think it's beautiful, baby." My mom kissed me on the top of the head. "Thank you."

I handed the drawing to my dad. "Will you fix it? Her face, Dad?"

"But it's perfect, Bea."

"Please?"

"Okay, let me try." He sat on the floor in front of my mom and me and held the pad of paper.

My mom made a funny face at him and then sat me on her lap. "You are my prettiest feature, Bea! Draw us, together, Richard."

"Would love to." He smiled and turned to a fresh page. He studied us as he drew, his large hands dwarfing the waxy crayon.

And then, suddenly, he stopped and looked away, out the large windows of the loft.

"Richard?"

"What's wrong, Daddy? Why did you stop drawing?"

He massaged the back of his neck. "Nothing, honey. I just feel a little headache coming on."

He crumbled the drawing. "I kind of messed it up. I'm sorry. We'll do a better one later on."

"You okay?" Mom asked.

Dad jumped up. "Hey, how about we take a break, maybe get some ice cream?"

"Yeah! Ice cream!" I ran to the door.

I remember walking with them hand in hand, down the streets of Chicago to the ice-cream parlor. I kept practicing my whistle, puckering and blowing the whole way, and finally, a tiny, teeny whistle came out of my mouth. I was so excited and celebrated with candy cane ice cream in a waffle cone.

And I don't remember my dad ever drawing after that.

"Bea, you want to come in and set up your easel?" Eve calls out.

"Sure."

"Kids, why don't you play in the sandbox? We'll call you in a minute for art."

"Yay! Art!" Maisy exclaims.

They tumble off the swings and run to the sandbox as I join Eve in the classroom.

"I thought maybe you could work on their ABCs—you know, draw a picture for each letter in the alphabet?"

"Okay. I think I can handle that."

"The easel is over there in the corner, and the paper is in that closet. I'll get the paint. We'll use primary colors today."

I pull out a pad of paper from the closet. A car door suddenly slams outside the school and then the car drives off—fast.

Eve looks at me. "What was that?" She runs outside and down the stairs. I follow. She looks around. "Wait. Where's Maisy? Who was that? What happened?"

Cameron fills a dump truck with sand. "Somebody took Maisy."

Eve rushes over to Cameron and Amanda in the sandbox and bends down to their level. "What? What are you talking about? Was it her mom?"

Cameron shakes his head. "Nope. It was somebody I never saw before. A car—a blue car—it took her away."

Eve looks at me, panic in her eyes. "Oh my god," she says under her breath and turns back to Cameron. "Are you sure, Cameron? You sure it wasn't her mom or dad?"

"It was a stranger," Amanda says, playing with a rubber animal.

"Bea"—Eve forces a smile—"why don't you come over here with the kids for a little while? I think I'm going to give Maisy's mom a call." She hurries into the school.

I take the pad of paper and rush over to the sandbox.

Think, *Bea*. *Think fast*.

I pull a pen from my hair. "Hey, kids, you think you can tell me more? More about the person who took Maisy?"

"I don't know. It happened, like, superfast," Cameron says.

I take a deep breath. "Okay. Um, how about we play a game? Have you ever heard of I Spy?"

"We have a book like that in the reading corner," Cameron complains. "We don't need to play that."

"Well, let's make our own book, okay? I'll start first. I spy"—I look around—"sneakers." I point to Cameron's shoes and draw a sneaker on the pad of paper.

"I spy *your* shoes," Amanda says.

I draw them. "What do Maisy's shoes look like?"

"She has sparkly ones, like your sweater." Amanda touches a bead on my sweater.

I draw. "Do they look like this?"

"Sorta." Cameron snorts. "But the sneaker picture was better."

"So, what did his shoes look like? Did you notice?"

"Who?" Cameron asks.

"The man who took Maisy."

"It was a woman," Amanda corrects me.

"Oh. Okay. *She*. What did her shoes look like? Did you see them?"

"She had on sneakers, like me. Cuz she was in a hurry. She was like"—he grabs an animal—"a cheetah!" He makes it run in the sand.

Amanda unburies a giraffe. "No, Cameron, you're wrong. She was more like a giraffe. She had a long neck."

"So you saw her face?" I ask, waiting for something to pop up in my head.

"Just a little bit," Amanda says. "And her hair was short, like a boy's, like Cameron's."

"Was not," Cameron objects. "It wasn't like mine!"

"Was, too," Amanda says. "And it was silver."

Looking straight into Amanda's doe-eyed face, specks of color flood my mind—a mosaic, fragments piecing together. I draw short, gray hair, a long neck, and dark, serious eyes.

Amanda turns her head sideways, examines the drawing. "That looks like her. Cameron, doesn't that look like the stranger who took Maisy?"

Cameron walks behind me. "Yeah, it kinda looks like her, a lot. And see?" He points at the sketch. "She doesn't have hair like me!"

A van swerves into the parking lot, and a panicked woman leaps out. "Where's my baby? Who took my baby?"

Eve comes flying out the school doors and dashes over to her.

Amanda takes the pad of paper off my lap and walks up to the woman. "She did. She took Maisy. Bea drew her."

The mom sinks to her knees. She holds the drawing, wipes tears from her eyes. "But . . . that looks just like my sister-in-law." She drops the sketch, pulls her phone out of her purse, and dials. "Grace? Grace, listen . . . did you happen to pick up Maisy today?" She listens, nods, exhaling with relief and smiles. Tears flood her eyes again, and she hangs up. "It's okay, it's all okay. It's her son's birthday party this afternoon—Maisy's cousin. She told my husband that she was going to pick up Maisy a little early. But I guess he forgot to tell me. I'm so sorry I put you through this."

Eve sits down on a bench, fanning herself as if she might pass out.

The mom turns to me. "How did you know to draw my sister-in-law? Did you see her?"

"No. She was in the classroom with me." Eve looks at me, puzzled. "How *did* you know it was her?"

I shrug. "I just listened to them—the kids. They told me what to draw."

A cop car pulls into the parking lot. Detective Cole charges out.

"I called the police," Eve says to us, "just in case."

"What do we have going on here, ladies?" He sees me. "What are you doing here?" He looks at Eve. "What's she doing here?"

"She works here, why?"

"Did she have anything to do with this incident? Did you?" He fires a look at me.

"Yes, actually, she did. She drew this." Maisy's mom hands him the sketch. "It's my sister-in-law. She's the one who took my daughter."

"I'm so sorry I called you here, officer. It was a misunderstanding," Eve adds.

"The little girl is fine?" He squints at me.

"Thanks to Bea." Eve sighs.

I lay a big, fat, triumphant grin on the detective.

• • •

Police lights flash and a siren blares behind me as I drive home.

Shit! I shouldn't have rolled through that stop sign.

I pull over in a diner parking lot and dig through my glove compartment, looking for my insurance card and registration.

I sigh. *Just what I need! A ticket!*

Tap tap tap. Sergeant Daniels stands at my car window.

I open it. "What are you doing here? You're not a traffic cop. If it's about the stop sign back there . . ."

"Forget the stop sign. I need to talk to you."

"You couldn't find a better way than to pull me over? Christ. You scared me."

"Sorry about that."

"Wait. Are you following me?"

"No, don't be silly, I'm not following you."

"Really?"

"You feel like a coffee, a pop?" He points at the diner. "I need to talk to you."

"Why?"

"Or would you rather talk in my car?"

Hell, no. "Fine."

We walk through the parking lot, he opens the door for me, and I sit on a stool at the counter.

"Why don't we take a booth?" he says, already heading toward one.

"Guess I don't have a choice." I sit down across from him. A girl, Emily, who I recognize from my physics class, takes our order.

Great, I'm sure she'll blab about me talking to a cop, start a new rumor that I've been arrested or something. "I'll have a Diet Coke, Emily, thanks." I smile, not getting one in return.

"Make it two," the sergeant adds. He waits for her to leave, then leans in toward me, lowering his voice. "So, listen, talk to me more about that thing you do."

"That thing I do? I told you everything this morning—but probably shouldn't have. It just happens sometimes."

"Detective Cole told me what happened at the preschool today—that you drew the woman who took the kid."

"Yeah, you should have seen the look on his face. Priceless!"

"How? How does it happen? How do you know what to draw?"

"I don't know, I just see it."

"It's . . . unreal how you drew him, my son, Max."

"So, do you believe me now? That sketch of the rapist?"

"Miss Washington, listen to me. This is important. Unless Willa changes her story and confirms that the face you drew is the guy who raped her, there's nothing I can do. I'm sorry. *She* has to be the one to make a positive identification, not you."

"But it's true about Willa. I'm not lying."

"I know you're not, now. I don't understand how you do it, but I believe you. That's why I wanted to see you—to tell you that."

"So you *were* following me!"

His face reddens. Emily sets down our Cokes.

I stir my straw. "I have a confession to make."

"Uh-oh."

"You know, we met before—you and I."

He nods with acknowledgment. "At that all-girls school last year. I was a detective—canine unit."

"Get out. You remember me?"

"Yes, I remember you. You're the one who hightailed it out of the room when Sally the beagle bayed at you."

"So, you knew I had drugs on me?"

He nods. "I suspected it."

"Well, why didn't you do anything? I mean, you could have had me arrested."

"We did do something, Sally and me. After the assembly, she sniffed down the school. Wasn't hard to find. A bathroom trash can—not too clever."

"But you knew it was me."

"I had a hunch but couldn't prove it." He puts his hand on top of mine—makes eye contact. "And it's a dangerous thing to act on hunches—you have to have proof, Bea, understand?"

I smile at him using my first name and then free-fall into his Caribbean Sea green eyes. And I'm without words—a first for me. A warm buzz vibrates in my belly, and it's not about Marcus, it's not drug-related. It takes me totally by surprise and stops my breath. I'm afraid to exhale. Afraid to move into the next moment. Neither of us breaks the stare. Neither of us breathes.

"You want a refill?" Emily asks.

We both exhale. The sergeant sits back in the booth. "No thanks," he answers, looking at his watch. "I have to pick up Max soon."

"Yeah, and I'd better get home before my mom calls the police."

"Funny." Daniels pays the bill and walks me out to my car.

We avoid eye contact. "Good-bye." He hops in his car and drives off.

"Bye."

A cop? Are you kidding me?

3 months 12 days 17 hours

Friday after school, my dad takes me to his campus for the tour. He is pumped, walking and talking a little faster than normal. I dress "properly" for him, wearing practical UGG boots.

I've been here, visiting him at work a gazillion times over the years, but he still insists on an exhausting tour of the full seven-hundred-acre campus. We finally sit on a stone bench, and he drones on and on about the Art and Architecture Building that stands in front of us. I try to stifle my yawns.

"I'm boring you, aren't I?"

"No, no. Not at all."

"Okay, I'll stop talking. Your turn. Why don't you share a little with me. Tell me what you've been doing at school."

"Not much, Dad. It's just school, not too exciting."

"Well, how about your art class? Are you doing anything interesting there?"

"Not really, no."

"But you're an artist. Aren't you working on something, drawing anything?"

"Well, yeah, Dad, I draw in my sketchbook."

"Can I see some of your work?"

"I don't know, it's kind of rough—you know, work in progress."

He laughs. "I understand. I used to be the same way. I didn't want to share my work until I was satisfied with it . . . which wasn't often."

I kick at a clump of dead sod, look at him. "I remember you drawing in our loft in Chicago."

"You do? That was so long ago."

"Why did you stop? You've never explained it. You never talk about it."

He doesn't answer, just stares ahead at the Art and Architecture Building.

"Dad?"

"Today is about *you.*" He stands. "Let's walk over to the studios. Come on. I happen to have a little surprise for you."

"Do we have to? You know I hate surprises."

"Too late. I've arranged for you to sit in on a life drawing class with one of the most revered art professors we have here at the University of Michigan."

I sigh as we walk to the Art and Architecture Building, down a long hallway, and into a cavernous art studio. Easels are arranged in a circle, and it's pin-drop quiet except for the sound of students drawing, erasing, and shading on paper.

"Bea, I'd like you to meet Professor Wright."

I shake the professor's crooked hand. He's at least one hundred years old and bent over so far that he can't make eye contact with me. "Welcome, Bea. Welcome to life drawing," he says to the floor.

They walk me over to an empty stool in front of an easel. Dad settles in on a chair behind me, smiling—so awkward. I hand him my coat and try to act the way any other seventeen-year-old who doesn't want to be here would act.

A model walks to the center of the room, and the lights dim. She disrobes and steps up onto a raised platform, lies down, and a spot lights her as she strikes a pose. With my charcoal pencil in hand, a visual drops in, nudges me.

This isn't the only venue where she strips. I could easily draw her in a cheap, smoky lounge, pole dancing. But I don't. I erase the bad girl out of my head and concentrate on the present—the respectable, probably boring good-girl side of her life—here in Professor Wright's life drawing class.

I try to capture every detail: her slender right arm draped over her face, her fingers dripping like icicles, her ample left breast falling to her side like a weighted sandbag, the indentation in her soft belly leading to her navel, the curve of her hips tapering down to bony knees, her arched foot, the bunion on her big toe. I draw it all. And have to admit, it's fun.

The session ends. The lights come up. The model slips on her robe and leaves.

Professor Wright lifts his head with effort and studies my drawing. He releases what sounds like a satisfied sigh, and I can feel my dad smiling behind me. The two of them then exchange an inordinate amount of nodding—a silent professorial language between them.

I thank the professor for his time. Hard of hearing, he answers, "It's five-thirty."

"You enjoyed yourself, didn't you?" My dad preens as he buys me a cup of coffee in the student commons.

"I did, yeah, sorta."

"Professor Wright, now *he* would be a great mentor for you, Bea. You'd learn so much from him."

"If he makes it through the year."

"What are you talking about?"

"Dad, he's ancient."

He laughs. "Don't worry, we do have a few younger instructors here. Would you like to meet a couple of them?"

"No, no, Dad. Thanks. I'm good—pretty pooped out." I stretch my arms. "It's been a long day. Can we go home now?"

He stirs his coffee, and we sit at a table. "I thought you'd enjoy this. See what could be your future."

"You mean, what could be *your* future—seeing me here. I'm not sure about college, you know that."

He sighs.

"Not yet, Dad, okay? I need some time."

"I know, I know. But I'm so proud of you, of your talent. I want to show it off—watch it grow."

"I'll always have it—the talent. It's not going away."

He nods. "It won't, you're right."

"Home?" I plead. "I'm hungry."

"Okay, we can go. But first I need to pick up some spray paint for your mother." He stands. "I pay for it, Bea, you know that, right? The supplies I bring home?"

"Of course you do, Dad. I know."

I follow him down a dark metal stairway in an old building off the Arts Quad. He jingles a ring of keys at the bottom of the stairs.

"Jesus. You have enough keys there?"

"I know. It's cumbersome, but it comes with the job." He unlocks the door to a supply storage room, and the smell hits me—the familiar and satisfying smell of paper, paint, and graphite. Shelves of supplies are stacked ceiling high.

"Wow." I look around. "This is like being a kid in a candy store for an artist."

"Now you know why your mother loves it here so much. This is her favorite place on campus. Do you know that I actually have to hide these keys from her?" He laughs and points to a door across the room. "That's the photography studio. You want to meet the professor?"

"I'm not into photography, Dad, you know that."

"Too bad. The students love him. You can take a peek through that window. He's young—I don't think he'll be dying for a long time."

"Funny."

"You sure you don't want to—"

"Daaad!"

"Okay, okay, it looks like we're running low on spray paint." He flips open a utility knife on his key chain and slits open a box. "Bea, help me put some of these cans on the shelf up there."

I help my dad, and we grab one of each color for my mom.

"This had better make her happy." My dad sighs.

• • •

"Hi, Bea!" Chris stands at my kitchen table—big grin on his face, his hair combed down flat and parted on the side. He's wearing an oxford shirt buttoned all the way to the top.

"What are you doing here? And why do you look like that?" My mom sits at the table. "Why is Chris here, Mom?"

"I asked him over for dinner." She smiles, sipping iced tea.

"When?"

"She called me last night. You didn't know?" Chris's eyes widen.

"He's a nice boy, Bea." Mom smiles again.

Dad walks into the kitchen and holds out his hand to Chris. "Wonderful to meet you, Chris."

"You knew, too, that Chris was coming for dinner? Why didn't you tell me?"

"I thought you knew."

The doorbell rings, and Mom stands. "Oh, good. That must be the pizza. Richard, will you get it?"

"Certainly, dear. And here's the spray paint you wanted."

"Thank you." My mom takes the cans from him and kisses him on the lips.

They're putting on such an act!

"Oh, and Bea, please set the table, would you?" Mom walks to the kitchen counter like nothing weird is going on.

"Whoa. Wait. Stop everything." I hit the pause button. "I don't understand. How did you get Chris's number? Why didn't I know about this?"

"I got it off your phone," Mom says as she tosses the salad.

"You what?" I yank the silverware drawer open. "You searched through my phone?"

Mom eyes me. "Why shouldn't I? You have something to hide?"

Chris whispers in my ear. "Bea, it's okay. She's nice. Chill."

I look at him like he's crazy.

"Pizza!" my dad announces, carrying in two pies.

"At least you don't have to eat her cooking." I groan.

"So, tell me what your interests are, Chris," Dad says as we eat.

"Photography, Mr. Washington."

"Oh, please, call us Richard and Annabelle." My mom giggles like a little girl.

"Photography—nice. And you two met last year? At art camp?" Dad continues his interrogation.

Chris nods. "Yes, we did."

"Did you hang out much together?" Mom asks.

"Um, no, not really. We hung out with different people."

"Of course you did." Mom refills his water glass.

"But we have art class together now, at school."

"I didn't know that." Dad sits forward. "What medium are you working with in class? I don't get much out of my little girl." He shoots a look at me.

"Well, we're doing a little bit of everything."

"Or a little bit of nothing," I add. "Our teacher doesn't know anything about art."

"No, she doesn't. But I'm excited about Monday," Chris says.

"What's Monday?" I ask.

"The field trip to the Heidelberg Project in Detroit. It's supposed to be fabulous. I signed you up for it, Bea."

This energizes my father. "Oh yes, the Heidelberg Project. Quite inspiring. They've taken a couple of city blocks in the ghetto and made sculptures out of run-down houses. It's not far from where I grew up. Fascinating."

"I know. I'm so excited to take pictures!" Chris is bonding with my dad . . . unbelievable. "Bea's going to pose for me in front of the sculptures for my portfolio."

"I am?" I ask. "That's news to me, like everything else is tonight."

"Great idea." My dad rubs his big, satisfied hands together. "So, what colleges are you looking at, Chris?"

I roll my eyes, picking onions off my slice. "Dad, give the college thing a rest, will you?"

My father ignores me. "You know, you should check out the photography department at my university. We were just there today, Bea and I. Bea wasn't interested in looking at it, but it's a great department."

"Yeah, it's a terrific school, but I don't know if I have the scores." Chris's face flushes.

"Oh, I think I may have some pull." Dad winks. "I would love to see your portfolio. And I could arrange for you to audit a class, if you'd like to, son." It seems my father is adopting Chris.

"Oh, how nice of you, Richard." My mom strums her fingers on the table, happy that she can butt in with *her* story. "You know, I attended art college, Chris . . . in Chicago."

"Really?" Chris asks.

I jump up from the table before my mom starts in on her saga. "Well! I think we'd better get started on our homework. Don't you, Chris? We have the physics test coming up, right?"

"Right." Chris obeys.

"But we didn't finish dinner," my dad says. "Chris is probably still hungry. Aren't you, Chris?"

"I, uh, I don't know. Am I, Bea?"

I grab one of the pizza boxes—the one without the onions. "We'll take it upstairs. Come on, let's go up to my room."

Chris stands and bows at my parents for some reason. "Dinner was great. Thank you."

"Any time, any time, Chris." My father bows back. "And let me know if you want to audit that class."

"Oh, I will, thank you."

I can tell Mom is seething, so I kiss her on the cheek before she makes a typical snide remark. "Thanks, Mom, for going through my phone and inviting Chris. It's been fun!"

It works, my unexpected gratitude. She sits in stunned silence.

I plop down on my bed and throw a pillow at Chris's face. "Why the hell did you come tonight? Oh my god, I told you about them . . . how they would be."

He sits down next to me. "Hey, dude . . . it wasn't that bad—*they* really aren't that bad. And to have a shot at U of M? Shit."

"What's with your hair, anyway?" I muss it up. "And you were frigging acting straight! Like you were my boyfriend!"

"I know . . . how'd I do, baby?"

"You're such a phony! And for chrissake, unbutton that collar. You look like you're choking!"

He slaps my hand away from his shirt.

I squint. "What are you hiding, Chris?"

"I'm not hiding anything."

"Bullshit, I know you." I wrestle him to the ground and pin his arms back.

"Bea, stop!" He squirms, laughing.

"What are you hiding? Tell me."

"Fine. Get off me and I'll show you."

I do, and he unbuttons his collar, revealing a two-inch hickey on his neck. "Ian McKinley." He raises his eyebrows twice.

"Get out of here! When did you two hook up?"

"We just . . . fooled around a little."

"How big is Ian's mouth, anyway?"

"Shut up. You're just jealous."

"Yeah, right, like I want someone chewing on my neck."

"Okay, I showed *you*, now you have to show *me*."

"What? I'm not hiding anything."

"Your closet! I've always wanted to experience Bea Washington's closet!"

I gesture toward my closet door. "Go at it, babe."

He opens the door and gasps, his hand on his heart. "This is glorious. Look at all these colors and textures . . . it's like a fashion treasure trove. Look at these jeans!" He pulls out the hand-painted skinny Levi's I wore in the Arb with Marcus *that day*. "When did you do these? They're amazing!"

"Last year, around the time I did your shoes. I haven't worn them in while. They're yours if you want them."

Chris holds them up in front of my mirror. "Really?"

"Yeah, they're ripped. There's a hole in the knee."

"That never stops you."

"Whatever." I shrug.

"Do you think they'd fit me?"

"Don't know. Try them on."

Chris unbuckles his pants, dropping them to the floor.

"Nice undies, Chris. Could they be any smaller?"

"Why do you think they call them briefs?"

"Ha. Funny."

He sits down on my bed, struggles with the jeans, trying to pull them over his calves.

"They're pretty tight but stretchy. Here, let me help." I kneel on the ground.

My mom pops her head into my room. "Gelato for dessert."

Chris stands and turns to look at her. The jeans are halfway up his legs—my head is level with his briefly covered crotch—and his hickey is full front and center, staring at her. She calls out, "Richard!"

Chris tries to hop away, falls to the floor. He pulls the bedspread off my bed and covers himself.

My dad comes in. "What's going on in here?"

I laugh my ass off. "I'm not giving him a blow job, Mom! He's gay!" I wipe my tearing eyes. "Tell them, tell them, Chris."

"She's not giving me a blow job, Mrs. Washington," he says, muffled under my quilt. "I'm gay."

Serves her right for messing with my phone.

3 months 15 days 9 hours

A yellow school bus drives us down the wacky blocks of the Heidelberg Project in Detroit: orange, green, yellow, purple painted houses; sculptures made of auto parts in well-groomed, empty lots. Two blocks of inspired outsider art surrounded by the poverty-stricken streets of East Side Detroit.

"This is frigging awesome, Chris!" I stare out the bus window.

It's a beautiful, sunny day in downtown Detroit, unusually warm for October, so warm that I'm getting away with just a jean jacket over a tie-dyed maxidress and cowboy boots.

We step off the bus and walk over to an orange polka-dotted house covered in stuffed animals. "This is called the Animal House." Chris laughs as he reads the plaque. "Good name for it, ya think?"

"What a riot! It's completely covered with stuffed animals—hilarious, even the roof!"

"Hah! Look at that." He points at a sculpture constructed of old abandoned doors in the middle of a field. Chris takes a picture of it with a vintage Polaroid camera.

"This is crazy wild." I look around, taking it all in.

"Hey, pose in front of that dollhouse for me." Dozens of doll body parts—legs, arms, and heads—are tacked to a plastic, discarded kid's playhouse.

Chris takes pictures of me as I swirl around the house. *Click, whir. Click, whir.* The film spits out of the camera.

"Why are you using Polaroid today, Chris? What happened to your digital?"

"It's fun, a different look for my portfolio, and I had some old film that was expiring."

I look out the window of the house. Barbie-doll limbs frame my face. Chris shoots.

"A Polaroid camera is also a good way to be discreet—you know, if you don't want a record of what you're shooting," Chris adds with a wink.

"And what sort of pictures do you like to keep discreet? Hmm? Pictures of Ian, I suppose?"

"Hey, I'm not a perv. Now stick your leg out the window—just your leg—and lift your dress. I only want skin and the boots."

"And you say you aren't a perv!" I laugh.

Click, whir. Click, whir.

That noise . . .

I walk out of the dollhouse and sit with Chris on the grass.

We watch the milky images come into focus. "That noise, Chris, that the camera makes—it reminds me of something." I pick up his camera and shoot at nothing.

Click, whir.

"Stop it—stop that, Bea. That film is expensive."

"Sorry!" I hand the camera back to him.

"Hey, let's go check out that buried car in the field." He takes off, running through a sculpted, ficus-hedged maze. "First one there gets the aisle seat on the bus!"

Chris chooses the backseat for the hour-long drive back to school. He goes through the photos. "These are so good, Bea—great for my portfolio." He flips through the shots of me—my leg, my foot, my pointing hand, my hair flying as I race across a field.

"Jesus. I thought you were taking pictures of me, not just *pieces* of me."

"Here, this one's for you. Bea in toto." He hands over a picture of me sitting in front of the dollhouse, deep in thought.

"I'm putting together an awesome portfolio, thanks to you, and am so excited about tonight."

"What's tonight?"

"Your dad didn't tell you? He set me up this evening in the photography class. I'm auditing it."

"No. He didn't." I guess he's honoring my "don't-talk-to-me-about-college" request. "Cool, even though you won't be marrying his baby girl. Very PC of him."

"He *knows* I won't be marrying his baby girl. There's no obligation . . . it's just an audit." Chris laughs.

The bus turns into the school parking lot. "Holy shit. What's going on?"

Cop cars line the perimeter of the school. An ambulance sits at the top of the football field.

The bus stops, and a female officer hops on. "We need you off the bus, now. Single file. Follow the bus driver. Once you are in the school, you will go straight to your homerooms."

"What happened?" I call out to the cop.

"Lockdown. Your school is in lockdown. There's been an incident. Now, please. Single file."

"Damn," I whisper to Chris. "You think he got another girl?"

"I hope not. This sure is creepy."

We file out of the bus. The cop gestures for us to keep moving. Another armed policeman stands at the doors of the school, waving us in.

I'm behind Chris, the last one off, and whisper in his ear, "Whatever I do, don't ask any questions. Just go along with it, into the school. Don't look back, okay?"

"What?" He starts to turn around.

"Shh . . . just look ahead."

Chris sighs. "Shit, Bea. Don't, don't do it . . . whatever it is that you're thinking about."

"Look!" I yell out, pointing to the far end of the parking lot, opposite the football field. "I saw something! Someone running . . . over there!"

"Where?" the female cop asks.

"He crossed the street! I saw someone running," I say, my hand on my heart, breathing hard.

The cop guarding the door shouts out, "Okay, everybody, into the school, *now*!" We rush through the door, and the officer runs toward the road.

I hook my purse over my left shoulder, crossing it around the right side of my body, and bolt out the door, turning the corner around the side of the school, toward the football field. I catch my breath, assessing the situation. The entrance to the tunnel that leads to the concession stand is about fifteen feet in front of me. I peek around the corner—the police are still checking out the "guy" and are now on their phones, calling for backup, I'm sure. I run as fast as I can, not easy with the cowboy boots, and slip into the dark tunnel.

My breath echoes off the concrete walls. I can't see a thing to the right of me—the door to the concession stand is closed. I sidle my way down the ramp blindly—don't want to use the light of my phone this time—and hope to god I don't trip or meet up with a rat.

Reaching the end of the tunnel, I feel for the door and turn the knob. It squeaks. I freeze. I wait but hear nothing, so I turn it again and push the door open—daylight rushes in at me. I fall to my knees and crawl across the floor, tearing the hem of my maxidress on my pointy boots. I part the gingham curtain, crouch underneath the counter, pull the curtain closed, and lean up against the safe, slowing my breath.

Stay calm, Bea. Stay calm.

I close my eyes, inhale through my nose, and exhale through my mouth, counting to four.

Something furry runs across my right hand. *A fucking rat! Ewww!*

The long tail slips away under the curtain, the rat probably as freaked out as I am. I'm totally grossed out, searching for hand sanitizer in my purse, when my phone rings—now set to Bowie's song "Changes." *Shit!* I shut it off just as he starts singing the fourth stuttering *ch*.

It's my mom—of course she'd be the one to blow my cover. I turn it to vibrate and freeze, waiting for the curtain to be yanked open.

But it doesn't happen. I hear a jumble of voices on the field—concerned, serious voices, and I crawl out from underneath the counter, peek around the corner, and see a cluster of cops, including Daniels, looking down at something on the fifty-yard line.

An officer holding a notepad talks to the sergeant. "A Beth Meyers. Sixteen. From Dearborn. Parents report she went shopping at the mall last night. Never came home."

Oh no. A sixteen-year-old.

"Wonder why she was dumped here?" the officer asks.

"He's playing a mind game with Willa Pressman," Sergeant Daniels answers. "The sick bastard. Okay, make some room. CSI's coming in."

A couple of men walk toward the crime scene, both

carrying camera equipment. The officers back away from the body, and I see her.

She is covered from her neck down to her feet with a dark blanket. Her hair is wrapped in something—looks like duct tape—flattening it. Her head is the only part of her that's exposed, turned, facing me. Her eyes are frozen, wide open like two solid marbles set into her skull—a blank stare out at nothing. Or something—the last thing she saw, maybe.

I clench my fists and scream a silent scream. *God dammit! I could have stopped this! I know I could have!*

And I hear it again. That noise.

Click, whir.

Click, whir.

Click, whir.

I peer out again around the counter and see an investigator taking photographs of her face, along with a videographer. The photographer's using a Polaroid camera and focusing, closing in on her face.

Click, whir.

That's it! That noise . . . the noise Willa heard before she was raped . . . it was a Polaroid camera! He was taking pictures of her!

I pull the photo out of my purse—the Polaroid that Chris took of me framed with plastic legs, feet, hands, breasts, and heads in front of the dollhouse.

Thoughts fly around and around in my head like rabid bats, and I sink back under the counter, open my sketchbook, and write:

Veronica at the Arb:
Torso

Willa:
Legs

This girl, Beth:
Head, her face

Legs, a torso, a head . . . and a camera!

Body parts. I shudder. He's taking pictures of their body parts! Like a sick photographic collage.

I peer at the scene again. The photographer has his back to me—wearing a baseball cap, dark hair hangs out from underneath.

No one would ever suspect him. He works for the cops . . . oh my god . . . that creepy police officer at homecoming, lighting my cigarette.

My teeth begin to chatter, and it's not just because of the dipping temperature. My legs cramp up. I stand. I don't care if they see me anymore. I watch the photographer walk away from the girl and lean on the hood of a police car as the ambulance rolls down the hill.

The girl's body—Beth—is placed on a stretcher and carried into the ambulance. It pulls away, around the track, and out the gate on the far side of the field. Silent—the siren not needed.

The cops disperse, walking toward their cars. I keep my eye on the forensic photographer. He climbs the bleachers, lugging his equipment. I run out of the concession stand and scramble up the ramp, fast.

The school doors open as I reach the top of the tunnel. Silent, shocked students walk out—their eyes pointing down toward the field. School busses idle. I fall into step with my fellow peers, and no one pays attention to me, the shivering girl with the hanging hem. And if they did, they'd probably assume it was a style choice.

I look around the parking lot and spot him. He's behind a gray van, placing his equipment in the back. I run to my car, start the engine, and wait for him to pull up in front of me. And I follow—follow him out of the lot and onto the road.

My phone vibrates. It's my mom again. "Hi, Mom." I talk on speakerphone.

"Oh, Bea, are you okay? I've been listening to the news all day . . . said your school was in lockdown, wouldn't allow phone calls . . ."

Thank goodness I didn't answer her call.

"Right, Mom, it's been horrible."

"They found another body, a girl?"

Her dead eyes flash in my mind. "Yes, that's what I heard."

"Bea, come home now! I need you home."

"You know, Mom, I'm pretty flipped out. I feel like I need to drop in on a meeting. I think there's one at four at St. Anne's."

"Bea . . ."

"Mom, it's okay. I need to go. I won't be long, I promise."

The van pulls into the left lane. I hang up on my mom and follow him.

He turns left. I turn left. He drives a mile down the road and pulls into a parking lot. Ann Ar-Bar, the neon sign blinks. I stop on side of the road and watch him, his head hanging low, walking into the bar.

I cross the street and follow him in. It's dark and smoky, a stark contrast to the sunny afternoon outside. But it's always nighttime in a bar—always time to drink, darkness lessening the guilt. I fall into a booth near the entrance and watch him sit on a stool at the bar, take off his coat, order a drink, and slug it back, fast.

I can't make out his face. His back is to me, and even if it weren't, it would be too dark to see if he had a cleft in his chin.

The front door opens, and a few cops walk in. I slouch and block my face with my sketchbook. I hear them order drinks at the bar—one of the voices is Sergeant Daniels's. "Give me a Stroh's."

A waitress starts walking toward my booth. Shit! I slip into the ladies' room before she gets to me.

I sit in a stall, on top of a cigarette-singed toilet seat, and think, *Okay, what's my plan? I can't let him get away. What if it's him?*

I dial Sergeant Daniels's number.

"Daniels," he answers on the first ring.

"Hi. This is Bea. I know you're gonna think I'm nuts, but hear me out, please," I whisper. "The photographer taking the Polaroids of the dead girl on the football field today . . . I think he's the murderer!"

"What? What are you talking about? Where are you?"

"I know it's him! You have to believe me," I whisper again. "And he's sitting at the bar with you, the guy in the baseball cap. Don't let him know you know!"

He doesn't say anything.

"Did you hear me? Did you? Sergeant . . ."

I hear footsteps and the door of the bathroom opening. A face, the waitress's face, peeks at me below the stall. "Yeah, she's in here," she calls out, snapping her gum.

Damn!

I jump off the toilet, open the stall, and the sergeant stands at the door of the john, his face set in a hard, angry stare.

I cradle my bag close to my chest as if it's a shield. "I know I shouldn't be here, but I had to follow him. I had to. I figured it out. He's been taking photographs of the girls. Willa's legs, Veronica's torso, and now this girl's face!"

His eyes grow wide. "What? Where were you today? What did you do?"

"I saw him! I saw him taking pictures of the dead girl, Polaroids, and it was the same noise that Willa heard—the noise from the camera."

"Get out of here!" the sergeant yells. "Now!" He backs away from the door. I hurry past him, flinching at his anger, and walk into the bar.

"Holy Christ! What's she doing here?" Detective Cole sneers.

I pause, looking back at the photographer, still sitting at the bar.

"Leave, Miss Washington, now! Unless you'd like a police escort . . . to the station," Sergeant Daniels orders.

"But that's him," I exclaim, pointing. "He's the murderer!"

The guy turns, takes off his baseball cap, wipes the top of his balding head, and rubs his cleftless chin. "What did she say?"

My knees go weak and start to buckle. "Oh, no . . . I made a mistake. A terrible mistake. I'm sorry. I'm so, so sorry."

The sergeant takes me by the arm and pulls me outside to the parking lot.

"What the hell are you doing?"

"I just wanted to help . . ."

"Well, you can't. Don't you get it? You can't help."

"Yes, I can!"

"Willa was the one raped, not you!" he snaps.

I take a step back, holding in tears. "You could have said

that same thing to Beth at the mall yesterday afternoon—and look what happened to her."

I sit in my car and hit the steering wheel over and over. I am so stupid! I'm idiotic! I wish I'd never gotten sober . . . this wouldn't have happened if I were still using. I can't take this anymore!!!

I dial his number. He answers. "Marcus."

I hang up—fast—and race to the meeting at St. Anne's, get my fix—the good kind—and end up crawling onto my parents' bed after dinner, in between them. They make room for me as they watch an antiques auction show on television.

My mom pets my hair. "This has been a rough couple of weeks for you, Bea. And now this girl at your school . . ."

"Mom, I don't want to talk about it. Let's just watch TV."

My dad puts his arm around me.

I settle in and listen to my parents bicker about what they think something is worth on the show. I allow the comforting banter to fill my confused, pounding head.

"Why would anyone bring that vase to the show? It's hideous," Mom scoffs.

"I bet it's worth a fortune, Bella."

"No. You're wrong. It's a fake."

"And how would you know that?"

"I just do."

I text Chris.

ME: sorry bout today

CHRIS: WTF? where did u go?

ME: chill.

CHRIS: it was another girl. u were right.

ME: ik

CHRIS: it was crazy being in lockdown. they wouldn't even let us use the john

ME: shit

CHRIS: almost did. they cancelled school tomorrow BTW.

ME: cool. where are u anyway?

CHRIS: auditing that class

ME: you went out? after what happened today? not like u

CHRIS: im not the wuss u think

ME: doubt that

CHRIS: OMG, the prof just came in. he's hot

ME: don't cream your jeans

CHRIS: im wearing yours

ME: LOL

CHRIS: k, i'm sending u a pic of him—he's to die for

The picture pops up.

ME: yeah, kinda cute but not my type—don't like beards

Another photo. This time the professor looks right at

the camera, at Chris. I turn my phone sideways, making the photo bigger.

His dark hair falls into his eyes as he looks straight at the camera . . . a square jaw, sculpted face, and a slight beard hiding what looks like a cleft embedded in his chin.

I stop breathing.

Dad peers over my shoulder. "Hey, look at that. Professor Woolf from my department. That's the photography teacher I wanted you to meet, Bea. Chris sent you that?"

I stare at the face on my phone and nod. Professor Woolf.

"Hah!" Mom exclaims. "I was right. You were wrong. The vase is a fake!"

"Guess you were right, as always, Bella." Dad sighs.

Ping.

CHRIS: his name is woolf, but it should be fox! ttyl

Woolf . . . Professor Woolf . . . James Woolf.

I scroll through the messages on my phone—the messages from the frat boys that night.

spotted winston howling at the moon tonite. i think he's coming to get u. —malcolm

malcolm gave me your # hook up? winston wants to watch 2. lol —dan

heard u give out. call me. —jock's trap

frat party tomorrow nite—winstons gonna b there with

a couple rats —manny
winston's smoking hot, baby —malcolm
check out woolf on campus. hes your guy. —J.W.
he vants to suck your blood —malcolm

I read it again.

check out woolf on campus. hes your guy. —J.W.

Holy Christ! J.W. James Woolf. Someone recognized the poster and texted me!

I sit up in bed, turn my back to the TV, and face my parents. "So Dad? Professor Woolf—that's his name? The photography teacher?"

"Yeah," Dad answers, absorbed, watching an appraisal of a grandfather clock.

"You know, I'm thinking that I should check his class out. Chris has inspired me lately with his photos, and maybe I should meet that professor."

This grabs my dad's attention—and my mom's. "But I thought you weren't interested in college?" Dad asks.

"Well, I don't know. I guess I could be, a little."

Mom lowers the volume on the TV. "Really." It's not a question.

"Tell me more about the photography professor, Dad."

"Professor Woolf? Well, he's a new teacher. I just hired him."

"Oh. So, he's only taught since September?"

"Straight out of Northern Michigan University. He's young, but he impressed me last spring in his interview."

"Last spring?"

"Yes, he was here right around your birthday. I remember because I had to rush him. I needed to pick up your cake."

April. Veronica. Arboretum.

"You know, Dad, they're cancelling school tomorrow. Maybe I could come by the university for a bit, look around again?"

"Of course, Bea. Nothing would make me happier. I'll arrange an audit."

"Dad, is it okay if I walk around by myself? It's kind of awkward when people know I'm your daughter."

"I understand."

"And could you give me the prof's schedule? So I know when he's there?"

"Sure. No problem."

I kiss him on the cheek. "Thanks, Dad."

The phone rings. "Hello?" Mom answers. Pause. "This is she." She turns the television off and gives me a puzzled look. "Yes, I can. I can tell you with all certainty that she's here, at home, with us. I'm looking at her right now."

Dad takes off his glasses. Mouths, "What?"

"Okay. Well, thank you, sergeant. Thank you for checking in." She hangs up the phone.

"Who was that, Bella?"

"A Sergeant Daniels from the Ann Arbor Police Department."

I swallow.

"He wanted to make sure that you were home, Bea."

I scramble. "Oh, yeah, Mom . . . the principal said they were going to make calls to some of the girls at school. You know, see if we're okay."

"Well, that's above and beyond what I would expect. There has to be a thousand girls at your school," Dad says, surprised.

"I think they're only calling juniors and seniors." I fake a yawn. "Well, I'd better go to bed. I'm exhausted. Good night."

My mom squints at me, chews the side of her mouth. "Good night, Bea."

3 months 16 days 13 hours

I wait on a bench in the Arts Quad. It's one o'clock—Professor Woolf's scheduled break. My tummy grumbles. I haven't been able to eat a thing since last night. I'm afraid I'll puke.

I have to be sure this time. I have to know, without a doubt! I can't screw up again.

The door to the photography studio opens. Students pour out. He's the last to leave, locking the door behind him. He wears a woolen cap and flips the collar up on his jacket, responding to the sudden chill in the air, and I follow him across North Campus, toward the student union.

He buys a prepackaged sandwich and a cup of coffee from a vendor and sits on a couch by a fake fireplace. He removes his coat, bites into the sandwich, sips his coffee, and stares at the fire.

I take a seat at a table across the hall from him, behind a potted plant. I open my sketchbook and peer through the plastic leaves at his face. I draw his profile: dark sideburns that lead to a trimmed beard on a strong jaw, long nose, full lips. I scootch my chair a little to the left to get a good look at his face—his eyes. They're set far apart under a heavy brow.

He looks up at a passing student, waves, mouths a "hi," takes another bite of his sandwich, and then . . . *whoosh*—a hand, a man's strong hand rushes in and takes hold of my brain.

It's there, right in front of me—reaching out, touching, stroking something . . . what is it?

I begin to draw dark, tangled, wild lines on the paper, entwined in the hand. My head throbs with the image.

Oh my god.

I look down at the sketch.

Hair. He's thinking of hair! My *hair! Reaching for it . . . touching it!*

I look up at the professor.

His lips curl like ugly, swollen worms, just like Willa described.

And he's smiling at me . . .

• • •

I pull into my driveway, right behind my dad. He kisses my pounding head. "I saw you today on campus, Bea. It took a lot of control not to say hi to you. You looked good, walking around—comfortable. Did you get to see what you wanted?"

"I guess you could say that, yeah."

Woolf's creepy smile flashes in my head like a shorted-out neon light. My nerves still raw, I shiver, massage my temples.

"Yeah, it's a little nippy out here." My dad rubs my arms. "The weather's crazy. Said it may snow tomorrow, can you believe that? It was in the sixties yesterday."

"I know. It's weird."

"Come on, let's go inside. I wonder what your mother's up to, what she's concocting." He laughs.

We walk into the kitchen. It's empty. No Mom, nothing burning on the stove.

"Guess we're ordering in," Dad says, taking off his coat. "Bella?"

We hear a wail, my mom's voice coming from upstairs.

"Mom? Mom, what's wrong?"

"Bella? You alright?"

We run up the stairs. My bedroom door is wide open, and my mom stands in my closet, pulling clothes off hangers, tossing shoes and purses over her shoulder.

"Holy Christ! What the hell are you doing, Mom? Why are you in my room, in my closet? And why are you making this mess?"

She doesn't answer me—she continues on, pawing through my belongings.

"Bella! What in god's name is going on here?"

"Mom! Get out of my closet!"

She turns. Her eyes are puffy and red from crying. "Why should I, Bea? Do you have something to hide in here? Do you?"

I'm confused as hell.

"Bella, what's this all about?"

My mom falls to her knees on my closet floor. "She's using again, Richard. She's using!"

I'm shocked into silence—incredulous silence.

"Bella!" my dad protests.

"Richard!" Snot runs down her face and spit sprays out of her mouth as she holds out two pills. "I found these in an envelope in her purse!"

The two pink pills—the ones Marcus wanted me to take that night.

Damn him! He dropped them in my bag!

"What are they, huh? Tell me!" she sobs.

"Oh, Bea." My dad crumbles down on my bed, his head in his hands.

"Shit, Mom, Dad," I stammer. "I don't know what they are—probably downers, and they've probably been in there for a while, from before. Flush them down the toilet, I don't care! I'm not using!"

Mom stands, points an accusing finger at me. "I knew something was going on! I knew it. You've been acting shady lately."

"Mom, please stop. You have to believe me! Please!"

But she continues on. "I've noticed a police car driving

by, looking at our house, the past week. And that phone call last night? From the sergeant? What was that all about, huh?"

"Mom, I can explain . . ."

"Richard, are you ready for this? The principal of her school left a message saying that Bea never showed up to her homeroom during the lockdown yesterday. He said that this is her second strike! She's already been called into his office once before. One more time, and he'll have to reconsider her enrollment!"

"Bea! What did you do? What's your mother talking about?"

"Yeah, what am I talking about?" My mother wipes her nose on her sleeve. "Give me your phone."

"No. I'm not giving you my phone!"

She yanks my purse from my arms, pulls out my phone, and scrolls through the calls. "Aha! You called him—you called Marcus last night! I knew it!" She shoves the phone at my face. "Explain that!"

"Mom, yes, I called Marcus, you're right. But it was a mistake. I knew it as soon as I did it, and I hung up. Look at the time—the call was one second. I didn't talk to him!"

"You called him, Bea!"

"Give me the cup—I'll pee in it, take a hair sample, whatever. I'll do whatever you want me to."

"You're damn right you will! I have a blood test scheduled for you first thing tomorrow morning so you can't fake it."

"Fine! Then you'll see that I'm telling the truth!"

"And I'm taking your keys." My mother grabs them out of my purse.

"What? My keys, why?"

"Because you're grounded, that's why! And don't try and sneak out like you used to. We're setting the alarm on the house tonight, and I changed the code."

"Dad, please." Now I start the hysterics. "Why is she doing this? Mom, not my keys, I need my car . . ."

"Bella, aren't you overreacting a bit? Let's wait for the test results."

"Overreacting? You want to see overreacting, Dick?"

She picks up my bedside lamp, pulls it out of its socket, and throws it across the room. It shatters against the wall. "That's overreacting!"

"Bella, come on!"

"No, *you* come on!" Mom's rage is now directed at my dad. "I almost lost her once, Richard! I'm not going to sit around ignoring all the signs right in front of my nose, like *you* did before, and risk losing her again! No. Never. Never again!" She turns to me. "Do you hear me? I can't lose you. I just can't." She storms out of the room, marches down the hallway to her bedroom, and slams the door shut.

I can see my dad thinking, trying to sort through all the rubble, the emotional debris in front of him—his large, praying hands poised at his pursed lips, his eyes closed.

"Dad, I need my car. Please talk to her," I plead.

He looks at me, his eyes dripping with disappointment, and he nods. "We'll get the blood test tomorrow. That's what we'll do. And then we'll see about your car."

He leaves my room and closes the door.

God damn you, Marcus!

A couple of hours pass, and my closet is back in order. I feel like a caged animal and have arranged my clothes by color, my shoes by heel height, my accessories alphabetically by the last name of the designer. I pick up the pieces of the broken lamp and toss them into the trash can. I remake my bed, fluff the pillows, collapse, and smell hot dogs and beans.

My mom must still be holed up in her room, because Dad is making his favorite supper—the only thing he knows how to cook—hot dogs and beans. He knows I'm a sucker for that dinner (a welcome relief, not having garlic), and I'm sure this is his way of trying to lure me down to the kitchen table to talk about the damn pills.

A tap on my door. He pokes his head in. "Franks and beans, Bea. Join me?"

"I don't feel like eating," I say, starved.

He walks in, his head hanging low, and picks up the trash can with the broken lamp pieces. "Well, I'll make a tray for you in the kitchen, just in case." He closes my door, and I hear him set the alarm.

I sit down on my bed and write:

I have to get out of this house somehow, get to Willa, to campus. She has to identify him.

But how?

I hear scratching. A branch of the sycamore tree lightly touches my window in the wind.

I walk over and peer out. She looks naked in the moonlight, having lost most of her leaves during the past month. Her limbs move gracefully with the breeze.

Wait. They have never alarmed the second floor—never had a reason to. There's been no way out, no trellis like at Aggie's, nothing to climb down on . . . until now.

I turn the brass latch on the window, unlocking it, place my hands under the lower sash, and lift it an inch. The wind whooshes in, hitting my belly.

Silence. No alarm, no siren, no hysterical, wigged-out parents running into my room.

I try and push the window higher. It sticks halfway, and I shove my right shoulder into the wooden sill until it creaks open. I bend down, and my face is smacked with the cold—and smacked with a solution.

She's right there in front of me, beckoning me—her farthest limb reaching out, luring me onto her mottled bark. I stick my head out the window, look down, and see the strong boughs spaced evenly, forming a ladder down to the front lawn—to freedom.

I hear Dad's heavy steps walking up the stairs. I shut the window and pull down the shade.

He walks by my room, pauses, and continues on to his bedroom, to Mom, and opens the door. Her bawling increases as he consoles, "Bella, Bella, it's okay . . . it's all going to be okay."

I tiptoe barefoot down the stairs to Dad's office and look for the hidden key ring—the keys to the art supply closet that he hides from my mom. I find them in a side drawer of his desk. I pass the kitchen, nab a couple of hot dogs, and creep back upstairs to my room.

3 months
17 days
5.5 hours

I wake up before my alarm and check the weather report on my computer. It's going to be gnarly cold, and yes, my dad was right, they predict snow—the first of the season. The sun is barely peeking through the heavy gray clouds in the sky, rising over the sleepy city of Ann Arbor.

I put on a large fleece sweatshirt, a pair of jeans, a drab ecru down parka with a hood, and my UGG boots.

Staring in the mirror at the dowdy reflection in front of me, I kick off the UGGs and pull on my "don't fuck with me" boots. I have to. There are times in a girl's life when fashion trumps common sense, and this is one of them.

I lock my bedroom door, strap on a green leather Coach backpack, and walk over to the window. The sycamore glistens with early-morning dew—not yet frozen, I hope. I push the window open. A blast of cold wind, colder than last night, blows through my room.

I stick one leg out the window and put half of my weight on the gutter. It bends a little with my heel, and I realize it won't take my full weight, so I lift both feet onto the sill.

Scrunched and bent over in a squat, I look down at the ground. If I fall, the bushes will cushion me, and I'll end up with a broken leg or arm—nothing too serious. Mom will go nuts, but that's the worst thing that could happen.

I grab the end of the closest branch. It bends and cracks in my hand. *Damn!*

Hanging tightly on to the window, I stretch my right arm up toward a sturdier, heftier limb, but it's just out of my reach. I lose my balance for a second.

I regroup, squatting and thinking.

I'll have to leap to it. I can do it. I just have to. It's not that far.

I take a deep breath, count *one, two, three* . . . and jump—springing up like a crazy flying squirrel—and my right hand hooks around the branch (thank goodness for the ugly Isotoner leather gloves I found tucked in the pockets of the parka). I dangle, hanging on, swinging back and forth, and finally pull my legs up and over like an upside-down koala and start shinnying down to the main trunk of the tree. I lower my foot, reaching for the next rung on the ladder. The high heel of my boot makes contact, and I place my two feet firmly on a limb.

Some of the boughs give a little with my weight as I continue down the tree, but she holds firm; and step-by-step I descend until I can safely let go, landing solidly on my two feet, and press my hot, sweaty cheek to her cold bark. "Thanks, girl. Wish me luck."

I found Willa's address in the school directory. She lives a few blocks from Chris—it's about a two-mile walk. I figure it'll take me forty-five minutes plus another ten, on account of the stiletto boots. I should arrive there about the same time my parents wake up.

I can see his face—my dad's—knocking at my bedroom door with a hot cup of coffee for me. It'll be how I like it—with tons of sugar. He'll knock. No answer. Knock a little harder. Then yell, "BEA, OPEN THE DOOR!" Still no answer. He'll panic. "NOW! DO YOU HEAR ME, BEA?" He'll put the coffee down and kick the locked door in—not knowing what he will find, what he will see. My mom, tired, her face swollen from all the blubbering last night, will rush to his side, and they'll find the window open and assume the worst.

Maybe someday I'll forgive them for not trusting me—not believing me—after all the hard work, the temptations I've fought off to stay clean these months. But I can't think of that right now. I have to get to Willa and make my next move . . . Chris's house.

I stand at his bedroom window. Good thing he lives in a one-story house. I don't think I'd be up for climbing another tree this morning. He's sitting at his vanity, dousing his hair with gobs of product.

I knock.

Chris sees me through the mirror, startles, and sprays mousse all over the vanity. I wave, gesturing for him to open the window.

He does. "Shit. What are you doing here? You scared the poop out of me."

"Sorry. I need a favor."

"At seven in the morning, you need a favor? Why didn't you call? Or ring the bell? You know, I *do* have a front door."

"My phone died, and I can't find my charger, and I didn't want to wake anyone. Can I please come in? I'm freezing!"

"You're so weird, Bea. Yeah, come on in."

I climb through Chris's window and collapse on his bed, on his beige bedspread, looking at his beige rug and beige curtains. "Geez. I didn't expect your room to be so . . . vanilla."

"You came here to insult me?"

"Your parents don't know, do they, Chris? About you."

He sits back down in front of the mirror, finishing up his hair, and shrugs. "They probably know . . . I mean, look at me. But there's no way they *want* to know. It's safer for me to stay vanilla."

"That sucks."

"Yeah, well, I have to put up with it till I go away to college—won't be long. Speaking of vanilla, you look like shit this morning. What's with that coat you have on? It's something my mom would wear."

"Funny, Chris, ha ha." I hop off the bed. "I need to borrow your Polaroid camera."

"I don't have much film left, one pack, but sure."

"How many pictures in a pack?"

"Ten."

"I'll replace it, okay?"

"Why do you need it?"

"Um . . . I was thinking of joining the school newspaper club, there's a meeting this morning, and I thought it would come in handy—you know, taking crazy candid pictures of some of the students and publishing them in the paper."

"You? The school newspaper?"

"I'm giving it a shot, Chris. Clubs and stuff look good on your transcripts for college."

He raises an eyebrow. "College? But you're not interested in college."

"Well, I am now." It's exhausting, sober lying. Lying never seemed this tiresome when I was high.

"Excuse me, do I know you? Did an alien shoot down from space and abduct my friend Bea and replace her with a parka-wearing imposter?"

"I wish. Man, do I wish." I look at my watch. "Shit, I'm going to be late for the meeting. Better go."

He hands me his camera. "See you at lunch?"

I pause, look at my good friend, and know I have to lie one last time. I say, "Yeah, see you at lunch."

I climb back out his window.

Brrr, it's an insanely cold morning. I spot Willa's address, her house. Her car is in the driveway, and I take a tennis ball out of my backpack. Thinking every step through, I researched "how to open a locked car" on the Internet at two in the morning. It looked simple on the video. This sexy guy burned a hole in a tennis ball (easily achieved with a quick flick of my BIC in my closet—didn't want the set off the smoke alarm), then he pressed the ball hard onto the key lock, and the pressure from inside the ball caused the lock to pop open. I watched the video about a dozen times, mostly because of the guy, but regardless, I'm confident in completing the task ahead of me.

She left her car unlocked. What a drag! I toss the useless tennis ball into the street, open the car door, sit in her backseat, and wait.

The temperature must have dropped a good ten degrees overnight. Winter has decided to make its grand entrance in Ann Arbor, even though it's only October, and it begins to snow.

I look at the time. It's almost eight o'clock, and now I'm wondering if the next step in my plan is going to work. What if she decides not to go to school because of everything that's happened? But I sense it in my addict gut—she needs to get away from her parents, who are no doubt fussing over her, watching her every move. School is the only place where she can slip away and score, feed her habit.

Proving the addict in me right, Willa walks out the back door of her house with her mom and dad, carrying a water bottle. She doesn't look good. She has dark circles under her eyes, her hair is pulled back in a stringy ponytail, and her nose is red and running. She wipes it with her mitten. Her mom and dad's faces are steeped with worry—I recognize the look—as they watch her every step. She waves at them and says, "I'm fine. It's going to be fine. Don't worry."

I duck down in the backseat of her car. Willa opens the door, and I immediately smell alcohol. She probably raided her parents' liquor cabinet—the only substance she's been able to get her hands on the last couple of days. She starts the car and pulls out of the driveway. I lie down on the floor.

We drive along for about five minutes, and I feel the car slowing, pulling to the right, to the side of the road and onto gravel, and stop. I hear a bottle cap twisting off and Willa swallowing.

I figure it's now or never and sit up in the seat. "Hi." Willa shoots forward, hitting the steering wheel with her head. "Oh, hell. Are you okay?"

She turns around and looks at me—her eyes like those of a tiger ready to tear into a piece of red meat. "What are you doing here! Get the fuck out of my car or I'll call the police!"

I look at the bottle in her hand. "Go ahead, Willa. I'll pass the breathalyzer test. Will you?"

"WHAT THE HELL DO YOU WANT?" she screams. "Get the hell out of here, now!"

"No. You're going with me to identify the guy that I

drew. The guy who you described. The guy who raped you. The same guy who killed that girl the other day."

Willa tries to erase the words, screaming, "NO, NO, NO!"

"You have to, Willa! You can't wait any longer. You have to tell the truth!"

"I did! I already told the truth!"

"No, you didn't, we both know that."

"Get out!"

I lean forward, rest my arms on the back of the passenger seat. "I figured it out, Willa. He's taking pictures. Photographs. He collects pictures of body parts."

"Oh my god, you're sick!"

"This last girl—her whole body was covered except for her head, her face, her eyes. I saw them. I was there."

Willa puts her hands over her ears and squeezes her eyes shut. "Shut up! Just shut up! I don't want to hear this!"

I continue on. "And the girl before, in the Arboretum? Her head and legs were covered. The only thing exposed was her naked torso. Google it if you don't believe me."

"NO, NO, NO!"

"And you, Willa—it was your legs that he wanted. You remember being wrapped in something, your upper body bound in a blanket as he raped you—you told me that, and it's how the boys found you. And you said you heard a whirring noise and a clicking. Right?"

"I never said anything to you. You're making this all up!"

"God dammit! Listen to me! What you heard was a camera—a Polaroid camera. He was taking pictures of you, of your legs, to add to his collection."

"GO AWAY! PLEASE, LEAVE ME ALONE!" She opens the car door and starts to run.

I bolt from the car and call out to her, "No! I'm *not* going to leave you alone, Willa." She keeps running. "Fine. Run away. But I'm just going to follow you." I sit in the driver's side of her car, close the door, and turn the key. The engine starts.

Willa stops running, looks back. "Don't you fucking steal my car! Give me my keys!" She walks toward me, slips, and falls on her butt.

I load the packet of film into Chris's Polaroid camera and open the window. I aim and shoot.

Click, whir. Click, whir.

She looks up at me, her eyes crazed with terror.

"Is that the noise?" I ask Willa. I continue to shoot photo after photo. "Is that it? What you heard?"

Willa covers her ears with her hands. "Stop it! Stop that noise! Oh my god, that sound!"

I don't stop.

Click, whir. Click, whir.

The squares of the developing pictures spit out of the camera, through the open window, and onto the snowy gravel.

"Please . . . please stop!" Willa buries her puffy face in her knees. Her head bobs up and down as she sobs.

I put the camera down and say, “Listen to me. I know who he is. I saw him yesterday. He’s a photography teacher at U of M. You’re going to come with me, to his studio, and identify him.”

Willa looks up at me, terrified. “I can’t, I can’t. He’ll kill me if he sees me. He’ll kill me this time—I know it!”

“He won’t see you, Willa—we’ll just take a quick look. That’s it. And then we’re out.”

Her whole body trembles.

“There’s a reason you’re alive, Willa, a reason why you survived, why you didn’t die. Did you ever think of that?”

Tears roll down her cheeks and her nostrils flare as she breathes in deeply. She wipes her eyes and nose with her mitten. “Okay, okay,” she concedes.

The snow is now accumulating on the pavement as I drive her car to campus. Willa finishes off the bottle of vodka. She is silent, her eyes set on the road ahead of us.

I stop on Bonisteel Boulevard, turn my blinker on, and we wait. The rhythmic clicking fills the car.

“He’s a photography professor. Teaches a class in a studio basement near the Art and Architecture Building—over there.” I point.

Willa instinctively ducks down. I toss her my backpack.

“What’s this for?” she asks.

“Open it up. There’s a hat in there. Put it on.”

Willa pulls out a floppy, chocolate brown, boho-style hat.

She makes a face. “This?”

"Yes, that. Tuck your hair up in it. There are sunglasses in the side pocket—put those on, too."

Willa digs around and finds a pair of oversized, round Dior shades. "They're huge!" she complains.

"Are you kidding me?"

She puts the sunglasses on and pulls the floppy hat down, covering her hair. I drive into an alley behind the building and park. "He won't even see you. We'll be in and out before you know it."

Willa stares ahead.

"Look at me, Willa."

She does.

"Everything is going to be okay. I won't let anything happen to you, do you understand? I won't let him hurt you."

She nods.

I fasten my hair with a couple of pens and pull up the hood of my parka. "Okay, let's go."

Willa steps out of the car like a zombie and follows me into the building, to the back stairway—the dark metal stairway to the art supply room.

I look at the time. "His first class of the day is almost over. There's a window you can look through. You don't have to go in. Trust me, this will be fast." She takes my hand and follows me down the metal stairs. The high heels of my boots click on the steps, so I tiptoe. One stair at a time. One breath at a time.

We reach the bottom, and I sift through the dozens of

keys on the ring. "Shit. Which one is it?" Using the utility knife as a starting point, I try key after key. Seconds tick by. *Damn. I didn't plan on this glitch.*

"Let's go. I don't want to do this anymore," Willa whimpers.

Finally, a key fits in the lock, I turn it, and the door opens. "Aha!" I drop the ring in my bag, and we enter the room.

I walk over to the window and look through the scratched glass. Class is still in progress, and Professor Woolf is at the front of the room. He's wearing that woolen cap again and, coupled with his beard, it makes me worry that Willa won't be able to identify him. He leans down, helping out a student, a pretty girl, and smiles his creepy smile at her.

"Willa, take a quick peek. Don't make a sound, just nod if it's him and we're out of here—up the stairs, and we'll let the police handle it. Okay? You got that?"

Willa takes a deep breath and looks through the window, in and around the studio.

"Well?" I whisper.

"I can't tell yet." She lowers the sunglasses down her nose.

I join her at the window.

Class is over. Students gather their backpacks, their coats. Woolf nods good-bye. He takes off his cap, scratches his head, and looks up at the clock. His thick, black hair falls down in his face.

Willa sucks in an obscene amount of air, jerks back, and screams, "OH MY GOD IT'S HIM!"

Hyperventilating, her chest heaves up and down as she runs out of the supply room, slams the door shut, and flies up the stairs.

I rush to the closed door. *Shit.* The doorknob doesn't turn. I push on it with all my weight. It won't budge; it's locked. I shove my hand into my backpack, searching for the key ring, and pull out the keys to Willa's car. "Damn!"

The door to the studio creaks open. Professor Woolf pokes his head in. "May I help you?"

I feign innocence, thinking fast, trying to stay calm. "I was just looking for some, um . . . art supplies . . . because I'm an artist and am getting some stuff for my professor. Professor Wright, you know him?"

"Of course I know him. So you're a student of his?" He stuffs his hands into the front pockets of his jeans and leans against the door.

I nod. "Yeah, I am . . . life drawing. The door closed behind me. No big deal. I'll be out of here soon."

"I heard a scream. Are you okay?" He takes a step closer to me.

"Oh, that . . . I stubbed my foot on the shelf." I rub my left boot. "Ouch. I'm so sorry if I disturbed your class."

"No worries. I just dismissed them. They're leaving now."

"Oh, okay. I guess I'll take these." I grab a couple of random charcoal pencils and pens. "Yeah, I think this is what I need. And if it's okay, I'll just leave through your studio, with the other students."

The professor reaches out and lowers the hood of my parka. "You seem to have a few pens stuck in your hair." He smiles. "You sure you need more?" He touches my hair. "You have wonderful hair, you know that?"

I sidestep around him.

"What's wrong? You don't like your hair? Or people touching it? Or just me touching it."

I put the pens back on the shelf. "You know, you're right, I don't need these. I have enough. I think I'll go now."

He gestures with his arm, welcoming me into the classroom.

Willa was right. He's repulsively charming.

I walk into the studio. The students are gone; the room is empty. I cross in a hurry toward the stairs to the Arts Quad at the far side of the room.

"Why are you in such a rush?" he asks, following me.

"I'm late for class."

Professor Woolf hustles ahead of me and blocks the stairs. "Why don't you stay a little longer? My next class isn't until noon. You say you're an artist? I would love to see your work."

"Maybe another time . . . I'm really late."

He gives me a look, the steely-eyed look that Willa described—the look that I saw in my head, the look that I drew on the page. "I think this is the perfect time."

I back up, turn, and run to the supply room, throwing my total body weight into the steel portal. Nothing—it won't open. I dump the contents of my backpack on the ground, bend down, and take hold of the key ring.

Professor Woolf picks up the flyer that fell out of my bag—the flyer I drew of him, the WANTED poster. "Interesting rendering. Looks just like me, don't you think? I mean minus the facial hair. Thank god I grew this beard and covered the cleft."

I face the door. My hands shake as I fumble with the keys.

"Thankfully the flyers weren't up for long. Nice of the police to help me out like that." He quickly reaches around me, grabs the ring out of my hand, and throws it across the room. It jangles to the floor. And then he leans in, his body pressing into my back, and whispers in my ear, "We had a smoke together. Homecoming. It was nice."

The creepy police officer in the tunnel . . . oh shit!

"That was the first time I saw you—selling popcorn at the game—this girl with amazing, wild, sexy hair. Isn't it odd how things work out? I went there to finish off that bitch, and then I saw you—your hair. I had to get to you somehow. I followed you home, remember?" He pets my hair.

I flinch, pulling away from his hand.

"And there you were at that bar. Your hair caught on my jacket as you tacked up this poster. I pulled it right down. It was so nice of you to give me your number." He laughs. "Did you get my text? 'Check out Woolf on campus'?"

I turn and face him, try to swallow dry spit. "That was you? You texted me?"

"I did. I wanted to see you again. It worked, right? You

came to me. Yesterday in the commons and now today." He takes my arm, squeezing it hard, and pulls me toward a door next to the paint shelves. "I'd like to show you some of my work. I think you'll appreciate it—being a fellow artist and all."

He unlocks the door and pushes me in, pulls a cord, and a safelight dangles above us, illuminating a photography darkroom.

My eyes take a minute to adjust—and I wish they hadn't.

Papering the walls are Polaroid snapshots—dozens of photos depicting gruesome, awful images. A collage of women's body parts—legs, arms, breasts, heads. The images shoot through me like an automatic firearm.

I throw my head over a plastic sink and vomit. Woolf takes my hair out of its high-knotted bun, allowing the nested pens to fall, pinging, down onto the concrete floor, and holds my hair back from my face.

"Well, well. I didn't expect that reaction—I think the photos are rather playful. I gather you don't?"

"You're an animal!" I spit the words into the sink with my vomit.

"But a talented one, you have to admit." He roughly pulls my hair . . . *just like that asshole did in the Caribbean! Fuck this!!!*

I swing my right elbow fast, sharp, into his ribs. He hunches over. I uppercut his jaw and quickly rush out of the darkroom.

"God damn you! Why can't you behave?" He tackles me

from behind and swings me around, shoving me into a metal shelving unit. The cans of spray paint fall over—some tumble to the ground. He closes in on me, grinding his body up against mine, caressing my hair with his right hand, cupping my neck with his left, pulling my face an inch from his.

"I've been waiting for hair like yours—your magical, fabulous hair—to top the piece off." He laughs at his sick joke.

I spit an acid spray of bile in his face. He slaps me hard and wipes the nasty spittle from his cheeks. "She fought me like this, the last one. It's why I had to kill her before the photo. I wanted her eyes alive—alive in fear. But all I need is your hair, you bitch. Your life means nothing to me. I can kill you now, and it won't matter." He locks both of his hands around my neck, choking me.

I can't breathe. I can't swallow. I try to push him off of me, but he tightens his hold. I feel my eyes bulge with my racing pulse. My arms flail, hitting the shelf behind me, and I make contact with a can of spray paint. I get my hand around it—hit the lid against the shelf, knocking the top off, swing it around, and spray at his face, into his eyes.

He steps away from me, and we both choke on the toxic fumes. I cover my face with my hair, hold my breath, and pull can after can off the shelf, spraying an arsenal, a rainbow of paint at Woolf's face.

He falls to his knees, coughing, grabs my leg, and drags me down to the ground. He tears off my parka, crawls on top of me, and yanks the top of my jeans, ripping open the zipper.

No, no, no!!! This can't be happening to me!

I look around for something, anything to hit him with. My sketchbook is open, lying on the floor. I see the drawing of Chris's hand and my hand, together as one. I reach out, scrambling, stretching out my arm, pulling it, dragging it toward me, and place my hand on top of Chris's.

Help me, Chris! Help me, please, somehow!

Woolf slightly lifts his body, unbuckling his belt. I struggle to get my legs free, and my left foot hits something. It jingles. *The key chain. The utility knife!*

He pulls at my jeans, and I look over his right shoulder and see the keys on the floor near my left foot.

I hook the heel of my boot around the ring and slowly bend my knee, dragging the keys up the left side of my body, cradling Woolf's legs, and fake a sexy sigh.

He looks at me with his paint-stained face through swollen, crazed eyes.

I smile at him.

"That's more like it," he moans. "You might as well enjoy it."

"I know. You're right. Here, let me help you with my pants," I whisper.

He raises his body a bit, breathing hard. I place my hands at the waist of my jeans, twisting them down my butt, until I touch the keys with the tip of my fingers on my left hand. I hook my pointer finger around the ring, feel for the utility knife, and flip it open. "Oh, hug me, please. Get closer to me." I wrap my right arm around Woolf's head and pull it against my neck. His face is buried in my hair; his hand is between my legs, groping. I lift the knife, above his back, and stab down hard, into his ribs.

Woolf screams and rolls off me. I pull up my pants, jump up, and am free to run. But first I kick him hard in the groin with my "don't fuck with me" boots and dedicate it to Willa and Veronica and Beth and all the other girls pinned on his darkroom wall. He curls up into a ball, howling in pain like a sick, lame wolf.

I pick up my sketchbook, kiss Chris's hand, and run out of the room, through the studio, up the stairs, and out the front door.

A blast of cold air hits my face as I see a half dozen black and whites gathered in the Arts Quad, parked in front of the studio. Officers are crouched, guns pointed. Sergeant Daniels charges toward the door.

He gestures for his men to hold fire. I run to him and collapse in his arms.

"Bea! Are you okay? Are you hurt? Talk to me!"

I shake my head no, shivering, lapping up the fresh air. "I'm not hurt. He's down there . . . in the basement. There's another stairway in the back. Please, please get him. Fast!"

Daniels shouts out orders to his men. "Down the stairs now! And cover the alley!"

I sputter, "Where is she? Is she okay? Where is Veronica? I have to see her, I have to know she's alright."

"Veronica? What are you talking about, Bea?" Daniels asks.

"I meant Willa! Oh my god, is she okay? Tell me, please!"

"Bea . . . Bea, look at me. Look at me now!" I do, but my body won't stop trembling. "Willa is fine—she called us immediately. Told us where you were. She's safe—Detective Cole took her to the station. But why did you say Veronica?"

I burrow into his shoulder, into his jacket, staining it with my tears. "I can't tell you. It's horrible . . . just too horrible."

He pets my head. "It's okay. It's all okay."

"I could have helped her. I . . . I was there. She was calling out to me."

"Veronica? Are you talking about the girl in the Arb?"

I cling to his sleeve, burying my head deeper into his armpit, trying to hide. "I wasn't far from her; I was near the bridge. I heard her, but I was too messed up to help."

"Oh, Bea." His arms wrap around me. "Is that what you believe? What you believed all this time?"

"It's true."

He rocks me back and forth. "No. No, it isn't true. You couldn't have heard Veronica. Her body was dumped there, at the Arb—she was killed somewhere else."

I look up at him, wipe my nose. "What? But who was it, then? Who was calling for help?"

Daniels puts his cheek against mine and whispers, "Maybe it was you, Bea. Maybe it was you."

Professor Woolf is dragged out of the studio by the cops. His hands are cuffed behind his back, his face painted in swirls of fluorescent colors.

"I didn't know you could paint, too."

I muster up a faint smile. "I did good, didn't I? Catching him?"

He wipes my tears with his scarf. "Yes, you did good. Stupid, but good."

"Bea, Bea, oh my god, Bea!"

I look up. She is running toward me. The cops have cordoned off the street and try to hold her back, but they don't know my mom. She tussles with them, kicking, barreling through like a Pamplona bull, calling and screaming out to me. "Bea, my baby, Bea!" My dad is not far behind her, following as she paves the way.

I am swallowed up in my parents' arms.

"Cut it off! I want it all cut off!" I yell.

"What are you talking about, baby?" Mom asks.

"My hair. I want it gone! Off my head, out of my life!"

3 months 20 days 16 hours

Willa was at the station waiting for me. I held her shaky hand as she positively identified Professor Woolf from behind a two-way mirror.

"You're going to be okay. It's going to be hard, but you're strong. You can do it, Willa."

Her bottom lip quivered as she looked at me with doubtful, scared eyes and walked away with her stunned parents.

She hasn't been back at school. Chris heard from some of the girls on the cheerleading squad that she's in a local rehab facility. The rumor is that she'll continue on an outpatient basis and begin school after the first of the year so she can graduate with the rest of the class. She'll probably write one hell of a college essay, knowing Willa, with all that's happened to her, and nail her Ivy League dreams.

The police collected all the photos—all the evidence

from the darkroom—and Professor Woolf was charged with the assault on me, Willa's rape, and the murders of Beth and Veronica. He is in jail, denied bail, awaiting trial. They're also looking into his possible involvement in a few cold cases in the Upper Peninsula.

• • •

"It's good for the tree, Bea. It'll grow back stronger and healthier in the spring," my dad says, unable to make eye contact. He knows it's bullshit.

I sit on the hood of my car in the driveway, my knees tucked up tightly to my chest, silently peeved, watching the tree trimmers butcher the sycamore.

My parents were relieved, of course, that I was okay, smothered me with hugs for days, and then smothered me with questions.

"Why were you in the studio with Professor Woolf?"

"What's your relationship with that sergeant?"

"Why were you involved with this?"

I finally answered at one of our stupid family dinners and told them the simple truth. "Willa needed my help, and I needed hers."

They seemed to accept that, and the questions ceased.

Mom brings me a cup of hot cocoa and joins me on top of the car. "I'm sorry I doubted you, Bea."

"Yeah."

"We're proud of you," Dad says, leaning on the hood.

"Yeah."

"Is there anything we can do, say, to prove it to you, how sorry we are?" Mom asks.

"Yeah! Stop trimming the tree!" I yell. "I'm not going to jump out the window again." I point at them before they can speak. "Unless you make me."

"Okay. Okay," they take turns saying.

"And no more family dinners!"

My dad takes my mom's hand in his. They look at each other, eyes wide.

I start it first; can't help it. Just a little hiccup of a giggle.

Mom looks at me sideways, catches it, sputters; her hand closes over her mouth, trying to keep it in—she tosses it over to Dad.

He's not as subtle. He puts his big hands on top of his nappy head and blurts out a loud, raucous laugh. "Thank god! No more family dinners!"

We huddle and laugh. Simultaneously angry and loving, as always . . . and they silence the saws.

4 months
16 hours

Aggie rests in Forest Hill Cemetery. There's a foot of snow on the ground as I make the trek up the hill to her grave.

Agatha Clara Rand

I take a photograph out of my purse—a picture of Aggie and me, the two of us—my face visible this time. We're wearing bikinis, laughing, goofing off at a school pool party when we were sixteen—sober that day, I think. I dust the snow off her gravestone and prop up the picture under her name.

"Hey, Aggie, you know what? I'm celebrating four months today. Four months, sixteen hours, and"—I look at my watch—"twelve minutes. But who's counting?"

I am. Always.

• • •

"Do you think you could help me find the other one, Leila?" I hold up a white, furry mukluk boot at the thrift store. "I think it's pretty cool."

Leila laughs. "Let me check in the back."

I sit down on a bench and pull on the boot.

"I like your hair, or lack of it," Sergeant Daniels says, leaning against a rack of coats. He's scruffy and sweaty in layered running clothes.

My tummy does a flip-flop. "What are you doing here?"

He holds his hand out. "May I?"

I bow my head down, and he brushes his hand over my buzz cut.

"You don't do anything half-assed, do you?"

"I had my mom set the clipper setting on number four—pretty radical, I know. But it's grown out a bit—going to be like a mini 'fro. I haven't seen you . . ."

"For a couple weeks, I know."

"Are you following me again?"

"Following you? I never followed you!"

We both smile at that.

"I happened to be running by. This is my route, and I saw you in the window."

"You spotted me without my hair?"

Leila walks toward us. "You're in luck, Bea. I found the other boot."

"Thanks. Um, this is Sergeant Daniels. Sergeant, this is Leila."

“Sergeant?” Leila looks at me, raising an eyebrow.

“Ann Arbor Police,” Daniels says and shakes her hand.

“No. It’s not what you think, Leila. I’m not in trouble. He’s just a—”

“Friend,” Daniels says.

“Right. A friend.” I agree.

The bells on the front door jingle with new customers. “Nice to meet you—and Bea, let me know if you want the boots.” Leila walks away to greet the customers.

“You know, since you’re a ‘friend’ as you say, do you happen to have a first name?”

The sergeant feigns a sudden interest in a woman’s corduroy jacket with elbow patches. “I do, yeah, but I’m not interested in sharing it with you.”

“Why not?”

“Because you’ll laugh, that’s why.”

“Oh, come on. I promise I won’t laugh—pinky swear. What is it, a girly name like Leslie or something?”

“No, no, it’s not like that.”

“What is it?”

“It’s Dan.”

“Dan? Dan Daniels?” I burst out laughing.

“I told you you’d laugh.”

“Well, that’s just sick. What were your parents thinking?”

“They weren’t. They were, um, my mom was messed up when she signed my birth certificate, when she had me.”

"Messed up?"

"Yeah. She and my dad were both pretty hardcore drunks, and she signed my last name on the wrong line, where my first name was supposed to be. So there you have it. I was named Daniels Daniels."

"Oh, jeez, I'm sorry." My nostrils flare, suppressing a laugh. "Why didn't you change it?"

Daniels studies the lining of the jacket. "I guess I hold on to it like you do with your chips. It reminds me of what not to do. Keeps me in line, my name."

"I get it. Sorry I laughed."

He looks at me, squints. "You're really something, Bea. You know that, right? Special. And not just because of . . . that *thing* you do."

"Thanks."

Our eyes lock—again—for a good minute.

Leila calls out. "So, Bea, you decide on the boots? You surprise me—not really your style."

"I know." I'm still looking into his eyes. "Surprises me, too."

"Okay, well." Daniels breaks the stare and pulls on his gloves. "I'd better get back to my run. I'll see you around, right?"

"If you keep following me, yeah, Dan, you will."

He smiles, starts to walk away—turns back. "You know, you can call me, anytime, like if you need anything."

"Okay. And you can always call me if *you* need any help—like in catching someone." I smile. "I could be your personal Bea catcher."

His sweaty blond eyebrows push together and connect. He nods a couple times and laughs. "Right, right. My Bea catcher. I'll keep that in mind."

I watch him jog off. I take out my Moleskine and turn to my favorite page.

It's a drawing of me. A sketch I drew while sitting across from the sergeant during Professor Woolf's arraignment hearing.

He was thinking of me. I was on Daniels Daniels's mind.

I close my sketchbook, smile, and hug it tight to my heart.

• • •

Kicking the caked snow off the bottom of my fabulous new mukluks, I drape my coat over my arm and step into St. Anne's recreational hall.

We sit, hold hands—young and old, fat and skinny, pretty and ugly, male and female—all different, all the same, all as one.

Karin "with an *i* instead of an *e*" starts the meeting. "First on our agenda . . . Bea, you have four months today, congratulations!" The group applauds. "Would you like to share tonight?"

I nod and walk to the front of the room. Karin gives me a big hug. I look out at the flawed fellowship in front of me and take a deep breath. "Wow . . . four months today. Pretty damn cool. But, shit, it hasn't been easy this month, that's for sure. Almost every day I think about using, and I almost slipped up a couple times."

"Who hasn't?" Granny raises her knitting needle in the air.

"I don't know if you noticed, but I wasn't too crazy about you all at first." That gets a big laugh, especially from Hawaiian-shirt guy. "But you're all kind of growing on me, I guess. You believe in me—even when I lie to you. And when I'm here, inside these walls"—I look around the tacky room—"I find that I'm . . . myself. You've somehow, magically, drawn the truth out of me. The truth of Bea—and don't seem to mind her. And, hell, the coffee even tastes better."

The door creaks open in the back of the hall. I hear a faint, familiar voice. "Oh, sorry I'm late." All eyes turn as she sits in the back row on a cold folding chair—the same place I sat when I first came. She sits between a tranny and the trucker, looking beautiful as always but scared as shit.

Tears well up in my eyes and stream down my face as I see that Willa is wearing my paisley velvet coat. I'm so beyond happy that a piece of me has been there with her all along, keeping her warm, giving her comfort.

She takes a deep breath and looks up at me with frightened eyes. I nod with loving approval, and she says, softly, "My name is Willa, and I'm an addict and an alcoholic."

"Hi, Willa."

After the meeting, we walk out into the parking lot and give each other a big hug. I watch Willa drive off and am about to get in my car.

Beep. Beep.

I look across the street, and there he sits in his idling Prius, summoning me to join him.

Marcus.

ACKNOWLEDGMENTS

To my husband, daughter, and son, you surround me with an impenetrable triangle of love every minute of every day. I am so lucky and grateful to have the three of you. I love you so much.

I thank my mother and (late) father for your unwavering love and support throughout the years; for your creative, artistic genes; and for sitting patiently through years of plays and musicals. You were always the first to clap—and the loudest. I carry your applause in my back pocket and pull it out whenever I need a boost of confidence.

To my *huge* extended family: to my six siblings, thank you for staging the "garage shows" back on Asher Court. I believe the bug bit me then—or maybe it was one of you. Regardless, it was a great ensemble, and it still is. I send big hugs to my in-laws for making the life of a starving actress in New York rather easy and for your continued support, encouragement, and love.

Every writer should have an agent like the beautiful Lisa Gallagher. Her intelligent, copious notes, solid belief in me, and hard work brought me here today, typing these words about how unbelievably wonderful she is. Cheers, Lisa!

To the team at Amazon Publishing—Larry Kirshbaum, Tim Ditlow, and Margery Cuyler—thank you so much for reading my manuscript and loving it and for providing me with my editor, Marilyn Brigham, who continues to guide and inspire me through her keen second set of eyes; and for Katrina Damkoehler, my art director, who honed and shaped the work of amazing cover artist Sammy Yuen.

I am indebted to James Patterson, Steve Bowen, and Leopoldo Gout for reading my pages, encouraging me to continue, and slipping them onto Lisa's desk. None of this could have happened without your help.

Alvin Sargent, you took me seriously years ago as a writer and graced me with your wry, unforgettable advice. I've tethered your wise words to myself with superglue. Thank you.

To all my friends (you know who you are), reaching back to when I was a little girl swimming in the muddy lakes of Michigan till now, hiking the hot trails of Southern California, thank you for your ears, your heart, for sharing your own stories . . . you are my living Post-it Notes, reminding me, giving me the inspiration and courage to forge ahead.

And finally, to my dog and cat, the most loyal of all, who book-ended me every day as I wrote. They listened to every word written and still adore me. Go figure.